Dear Reader,

We have exciting news! The contemporary line Harlequin Blaze books you know and love will be getting a brand-new look. And it's *hot!* Turn to the back of this book for a sneak peek....

But don't worry—nothing else about the Blaze books has changed. You'll still find those unforgettable love stories with intrepid heroines, hot, hunky heroes and a double dose of sizzle!

So be sure to check out our new supersexy covers. You'll find these newly packaged Blaze editions on the shelves December 18th, 2012, wherever you buy your books.

In the meantime, check out this month's red-hot reads.

LET IT SNOW by Leslie Kelly and Jennifer LaBrecque
(A Blazing Bedtime Stories Holiday Edition)

HIS FIRST NOELLE by Rhonda Nelson
(Men Out of Uniform)

ON A SNOWY CHRISTMAS NIGHT by Debbi Rawlins
(Made in Montana)

NICE & NAUGHTY by Tawny Weber

ALL I WANT FOR CHRISTMAS
by Lori Wilde, Kathleen O'Reilly and Candace Havens
(A Sizzling Yuletide Anthology)

HERS FOR THE HOLIDAYS by Samantha Hunter
(The Berringers)

Happy holidays!

WITHDRAWN

Brenda Chin
Senior Editor
Harlequin Blaze

ABOUT THE AUTHORS

Leslie Kelly has written dozens of books and novellas for Harlequin Blaze and HQN. Known for her sparkling dialogue, fun characters and depth of emotion, her books have been honored with numerous awards, including a National Readers' Choice Award, an *RT Book Reviews* Award, and three nominations for the highest recognition in romance, the RWA RITA® Award. Leslie lives in Maryland with her own romantic hero, Bruce, and their three daughters. Visit her online at www.lesliekelly.com or at her blog, www.plotmonkeys.com.

After a varied career path that included barbecue-joint waitress, corporate numbers cruncher, and bug business maven, **Jennifer LaBrecque** has found her true calling writing contemporary romance. Named 2001 Notable New Author of the Year and 2002 winner of the prestigious Maggie Award for Excellence, she is also a two-time RITA® Award finalist. Jennifer lives in suburban Atlanta with a Chihuahua who runs the whole show.

Leslie Kelly
Jennifer LaBrecque

LET IT SNOW...

HARLEQUIN®
entertain, enrich, inspire™

ISBN-13: 978-0-373-79727-1

LET IT SNOW…

Copyright © 2012 by Harlequin Books S.A.

The publisher acknowledges the copyright holders of the individual works as follows:

THE PRINCE WHO STOLE CHRISTMAS
Copyright © 2012 by Leslie Kelly

MY TRUE LOVE GAVE TO ME…
Copyright © 2012 by Jennifer A. LaBrecque

Recycling programs for this product may not exist in your area.

This edition published by arrangement with Harlequin Books S.A.

For questions and comments about the quality of this book, please contact us at CustomerService@Harlequin.com.

® and TM are trademarks of Harlequin Enterprises Limited or its corporate affiliates. Trademarks indicated with ® are registered in the United States Patent and Trademark Office, the Canadian Trade Marks Office and in other countries.

www.Harlequin.com

Printed in U.S.A.

CONTENTS

LESLIE KELLY

THE PRINCE
WHO STOLE CHRISTMAS

To Bruce. Thanks for being my prince
and for giving me my happily ever after.

Prologue

ONCE UPON A TIME, in a faraway land, in a world called Elatyria, there lived a handsome prince who believed in true love.

This prince had been raised by parents who adored each other. Their lives were filled with love, joy and happiness. He had always looked forward to the day when he would meet his own soul mate, with whom he could share his life and his kingdom.

Unfortunately, though he tried and tried, the prince could not find a bride who loved him for himself. All the eligible maidens he met proved to be more interested in his crown, his palaces and his lands than in his person.

Growing discouraged, he began to cast off his royal duties and go out into the world to meet as many women as he could, looking for his one-and-only, forever love—and finding along the way a lot of one-of-many, for today lovers.

With his parents aging, and his kingdom needing an heir, the prince realized the time had come to settle down and do his duty. Relenting to family pressure, he agreed to make one last foray into the wide world in search of his soul mate. If she was not to be found, he promised to marry a girl his parents chose for him.

With time running out, the prince had one last hope, and one final place to go to try to find the woman of his dreams....

A magical city called New York.

1

"IF I DON'T COME UP WITH the money, I'm in big trouble."

Claire Hoffman had been trying to ignore her brother, Freddy, who had burst into the kitchen of her candy shop, ranting about his latest financial emergency. It was under four weeks until Christmas; she had a ton of work to do, and no time to deal with his histrionics.

But unlike usual Freddy's tone, he didn't sound cajoling and playful now. He sounded serious. Very serious.

Her hand shook, ever so slightly, but enough to sabotage the delicate lacework icing she'd been applying to a tray of tiny petits fours. She lowered the icing bag. "What are you talking about?"

Ignoring her for a moment, Freddy grabbed a café con leche truffle—one of her specialties—and stuffed it into his mouth.

"Freddy?" she snapped.

"I'm starving. I don't even have money to feed myself."

She didn't ask why. Freddy made a fair wage ushering at one of the theaters on Broadway, but whatever he made was never enough to keep him solvent between paychecks. Which was why she hadn't immediately panicked when he'd burst in a few minutes ago, looking for cash. She was used to slipping him a twenty she could hardly spare, knowing the money was worth avoiding the nagging.

But she suspected a twenty wasn't going to cut it this time.

"What have you done?"

He finished chewing, then looked down at his feet, scuffing them on the floor. It might have been cute when he was ten and, five years older, Claire was practically raising him, since their delicate, prima ballerina mother was so often ill. But it wasn't cute now that he was twenty-one, and a lazy, often unemployed college dropout who seemed happy to coast through life.

After he'd spent his share of their mom's life insurance policy, he'd started bumming from Claire's. Now that she had invested every penny in updating the ancient building her uncle had left her, and starting her shop, I Want Candy, she could no longer serve as Freddy's ATM. "What. Have. You. Done?"

"It shoulda been a sure thing. I mean, that race…"

"Jesus, Freddy!"

A flush rose up his neck, mottling his cheeks.

"How much did you lose?"

"Well, it wasn't so much the race…."

She reached for a truffle and bit into it, then grabbed another one. She needed to busy her hands so she wouldn't strangle him, and busy her mouth so she wouldn't scream.

"See, when I realized how deep I was in, I went to leverage what I had left on last weekend's NFL games."

He snagged a petit four. She snatched it back. *"How much?"*

He mumbled a reply, so softly she couldn't be sure she'd heard right. *Oh, God, please let me not have heard right.* "What?"

"Um…ten large."

"Tell me you mean ten oversize one-dollar bills."

He shook his head, looking miserable. "Ten grand."

The truffles threatened to come back up. For a moment Claire couldn't think. As if on autopilot, she reached for a nearby bottle of Grand Marnier she'd used in the truffles, twisted off the top and swallowed several mouthfuls. The liqueur burned a fiery path down her throat, snapping her out of her lethargy.

Setting the bottle down, she stretched her hands out and strode toward her brother, ready to choke him.

"Hey," he cried, shuffling backward. "What are you doing?"

"Strangling you. Your life insurance is paid up, right?"

"That's not funny."

"You think I'm joking? I am mad enough to kill you, Freddy!"

"I'm sorry," he squealed.

Her fury seeped out of her. "How could you do this?" she mumbled, collapsing onto a stool in front of the counter.

Of all people, Freddy should *know* better. But the fact that their gambler father had lost all his money and died of a stroke at fifty apparently hadn't taught him anything.

"I didn't mean to. Claire, you gotta help me. If I don't make good, the Rat King is gonna send the Nutcracker after me."

She gaped at her brother. "The *who* is going to send the *what?*"

"The Rat King's a bookie. The Nutcracker is his enforcer."

Torn between wanting to burst into hysterical laughter or scream, she stared at her imbecilic sibling. "The *Nutcracker?*"

"Yeah. He got his name because if you don't pay, he, uh…"

Claire waved a hand. "I think I can figure it out." Considering she'd often thought her brother needed to grow a pair, she wasn't sure the collector would be cracking much.

"I can't help you," she stated calmly.

Freddy's eyes rounded into saucers. *"What?"*

"I have barely enough to cover my expenses for the rest of the month. I'm counting on a big holiday season to make this place pay. My lines of credit are totally tapped out."

"You could rent the upstairs apartments…."

"No." The argument was a familiar one. "They're one step up from needing to be condemned."

"Come on, it's Midtown. People would pay five grand a month for the location alone. Screw the peeling paint on the walls!"

It wasn't just peeling paint. Her great-uncle Harry had left her the run-down property, but no cash. Her mother's life insurance had given her enough money to get the first-floor shop renovated, along with the apartment behind it, where Claire now lived, but nothing else. The upstairs units—two on each level, going up three floors—were uninhabitable. Squatters living up there had had the good sense to move out, driven away by the frigid air that poured through the cracked windows. Then there were the holes in the walls, the mildewed bathrooms and the drooping wallpaper. Not a pretty picture. Someday, when the shop was thriving, she'd have enough money to continue the renovations and make the whole building a lucrative investment. But not now.

The only way she could get any money out of this place would be if she agreed to sell it to the investor who'd been coming around a lot in the last month. Yet the idea of giving up her chance to build a future for herself made her heart clench. Especially if she had to do it to bail out her idiot brother.

Claire got so tired of taking care of him…of everyone. When their mother had gotten sick, Claire had been the one to nurse her. When her father had lost his money, she'd started working to help support the family. When they were both gone and it was just her and Freddy, she'd become a mother to a teenager, when she wasn't much past her own teenage years.

She was tired. So damn tired of being the caretaker. It had been such a long time since anyone had taken care of *her,* she honestly didn't remember what it felt like.

"Freddy, even if I would *consider* renting them, I couldn't get the permits. Everything above this floor is a ruin." Seeing him about to speak again, she threw a hand up. "And no, I'm not renting under the table. Legal trouble is the last thing I need."

"So what am I supposed to do?" he asked, sounding petulant.

She bit her tongue to prevent herself from suggesting that he grow the hell up, be a man and deal with his own problems.

"What about a payment plan?" she asked. "You could promise to give him a certain amount of your paycheck every week...."

Her brother rolled his eyes. "Bookies don't finance."

"You've got no other options. You have to at least ask."

If the "Rat King" said no, then she'd go into full panic mode and start considering selling organs on the black market. She could think of a few of Freddy's that could be spared, like his useless brain.

Otherwise...was she prepared to give up everything she'd worked so hard for to save her brother's bacon? *Again?*

Oh, God, she hoped it wouldn't come to that. She just had to pray that in this magical season of giving, the *rat* discovered he had a heart, and the *nutcracker* went on vacation.

But she wasn't counting on it. This might be the time for miracles, but Claire had stopped believing in those long ago. She'd never been the type to fantasize about some rich Prince Charming galloping in on his white steed to take care of all her problems. And she sure didn't expect one now.

"MY PRINCE, please reconsider. We can't possibly live *here.*"

Philip Nadir, crowned prince of the Kingdom of Selandria

of the Dry Lands, heard the dismay in the voice of his loyal but fastidious companion, Shelby, and smiled. "Of course we can, and we shall. This will do quite well," he said as he watched his bodyguard, Phateen—also called Teeny—enter, muscling a mattress through the doorway. "Perhaps we should leave that until Shelby clears away the debris on the floor?" he suggested, remembering the condition of the small sleeping chamber, which he'd seen on a tour of the building yesterday.

"Until *who* clears away the debris?" the man squealed. "Are you saying *I* should do it?"

"Of course not, my prince. But I can't be expected to…"

Quirking a brow, Philip stared at Shelby, who was almost as spoiled as Philip was *accused* of being, and harder to please. A cousin, Shelby had come to visit when they were children, and had never left. Most looked upon him as a servant; Philip called him friend. But he could be—how did they say it?—high maintenance.

"Do you want to go back to Elatyria?"

A rueful frown pulled at the other man's face. He had been adamant that he be allowed to come along on this quest— Philip's last chance to find a woman he could love, who would love him for himself—but so far he wasn't acting very happy about it.

"No, Your Highness. But surely a scullery wench…"

"We're supposed to be poor, struggling students. Poor people can't afford to hire, uh, I believe the term is *cleaning* ladies."

Shelby huffed. Never having been to this world before, he was having difficulty adjusting, daunted by the tall buildings, the crowds, the frantic pace and the lack of subservience.

Philip, on the other hand, was having the time of his life.

Though he'd been raised in Elatyria, he was fond of Earth, a world that somehow existed, as his father's sorcerer described it, "One plane over from our reality." He had been here a few times before, but only with guards and servants.

He had never been one to complain about the weight of his responsibilities, and had been the first to appreciate the benefits that came with being the bachelor prince of one of the richest kingdoms in his world. But until now he'd never understood the joy of walking down a public thoroughfare and being jostled by strangers, or of flipping a worthless piece of paper at someone and being given something called a hot dog. Escaping his usual retinue for this quest to find his bride was giving him the chance to be completely free. And what better time than during one of the most popular holiday seasons of this world? New York was bedecked with lights and decorations, and populated by happy, smiling people. He loved it already.

Shelby toggled a button on the wall that was supposed to send light flooding out of the ceiling. "Why won't this work?"

"Hmm." Philip walked over and tried it himself. Nothing happened.

Though it was only late afternoon, the shadows of evening were drawing close. The air was chilly, so apparently the heating apparatus wasn't working. He wasn't used to cold weather, being from a dry, desertlike kingdom, but knew he could "rough it," as the locals said, for a night or so. But Shelby was another story.

"I'll go downstairs and talk to the innkeeper," he declared, wanting to confirm a few more details with that man, a Mr. Freddy Hoffman. Philip had thought Hoffman would be here today for their move-in. But he had seen neither hide nor hair of him since yesterday, when Philip had met him and paid a month's rent, plus something called "security," for both the second-floor living units, one for him, one for Shelby and Teeny.

"Do start working on the debris, won't you?" Philip said as he exited.

He walked down the dingy corridor to the back stairway. If he wasn't mistaken, Mr. Hoffman had said this stairwell led to the first-floor shop and the owner's apartment.

Moving carefully down the steps, he frowned, feeling the sag of the boards beneath his feet and hearing their noisy creaks. He reached the bottom level, coming to a long, narrow hallway, shadowy and cluttered. At the far end was a door that led outside to a back alley. In the opposite direction was the front entrance to the building. In between were two other doors, the nearest marked Private. Another, closer to the front, was marked I Want Candy: Deliveries.

From behind it he could hear music. The sound grew louder as he approached, so he knocked once, then pushed the door open.

The music was much louder in here, and the smooth-voiced female singer was purring to someone she called Santa Baby, inviting him to leave her gifts. Philip placed the reference, though he was unaccustomed to hearing seductive songs about Santa Claus, a character most thought an American invention. But who, Philip knew, actually resided in one of the icy northern kingdoms of Elatyria.

Suddenly, that sultry tone was made sultrier by the addition of another female voice. He couldn't help moving into the main part of the large kitchen, intrigued by the throaty, feminine sound. He didn't see a duo of women performing, only the one. The instrumentation, and the first voice, emerged from a small electronic box. The other singer stood in front of a tall counter that was laden with sweets, and was singing along as she worked.

Singing very well. Working very hard.

Looking utterly beautiful.

Philip was used to the perfection of princesses who would

never be seen without elaborately coiffed hair or elegant, bejeweled gowns. Who would never allow a potential suitor to behold them in a state like this. But never had he seen a woman who so immediately appealed to him on such a deep, visceral level.

Her mass of dark brown hair strained to free itself from a haphazard bun, a few tendrils brushing her high cheekbones. The face was arresting—not perfect, he supposed, but very attractive, with soft cheeks, a pert nose, and a wide, sensuous mouth. Her eyes were deep-set, green or blue, and ringed with thick, dark lashes, and her high brow furrowed as she concentrated on a tricky bit of work she was doing on a delicacy before her.

She continued to sing, and as she finished dabbling some icing on a sweet, she added a toss of her head and a swivel of her hips in time with the beat.

The toss caught his attention, making him wonder if all that glorious hair would tumble down about her shoulders. The swivel *kept* his attention, for he hoped it would be repeated.

Because, oh, did the woman have swiveling hips. She was incredibly curvaceous. The smock she wore over her simple clothing emphasized the smallness of her waist compared to the curve of her hips and backside. Not to mention the fullness of her breasts, the tops of which peeked above the apron.

She was also tall—very tall, compared to most women in his world—and if they were to stand facing each other, their noses would almost touch. Other parts would line up equally well. Some of those other parts reacted to that thought, until his newly purchased "Jean" pants—who Jean was and why men's pants were named after her, he did not know—began to tighten.

The stranger crooned even louder, and Philip couldn't help thinking about what he'd like to slip her under her tree. Before he could clear his throat to warn her of his presence, she turned to retrieve something, and saw him standing there watching her.

"Oh, my God!" she cried, dropping a chocolate-smeared spoon onto the counter. Immediately backing up, she almost tripped over her own feet, and began looking around the room, as if wanting a sharp implement with which to defend herself.

"My apologies. I didn't mean to startle you," he said, lifting both hands in a gesture he'd learned meant *No harm, no foul,* though what that expression meant, exactly, he wasn't sure. Still, it seemed appropriate for the situation.

"Who are you? What do you want?"

"I'm seeking Mr. Hoffman. Freddy Hoffman."

She studied him, her gaze dropping to his shoulders and chest, assessing. Well used to female appreciation, Philip allowed a slight smile to begin curving his lips.

She, on the other hand, began to frown. In fact, a scowl tugged at her beautiful face, as if she were most displeased with his appearance. That, he was *not* used to. One of his brows shot up in surprise. Though not a vain man, he was certainly not accustomed to disdain from women.

"You're *him,* right?"

"I believe you mean to say 'You're he.'"

"Are you seriously lecturing me on grammar right now?"

"'Twasn't a lecture," he said, amused by her disgruntled tone. "Merely a correction."

"Jeez, I'm being *corrected* by a thug."

"A… What did you call me?"

"A thug." She spat out the word. "That's what you are, isn't it? Oh, you might call yourself an enforcer, or a bill collector, but we both know the truth, don't we, Mr. Nutcracker?"

Nutcracker? What an unusual name.

Though Philip was very confused now, he had to admit

the sparkle in the woman's eyes and the flush of color on her cheeks were most becoming. If anything, she was even prettier now that she was indignant. Though what had caused the indignation, he didn't know. Perhaps it was the aforementioned Mr. Nutcracker.

"You should be ashamed of yourself," she said, moving closer as she scolded. Close enough for him to see her eyes and note they were neither blue nor green, but rather a combination of the two. They brought to mind the color of the Great Elatyrian Sea under a sunny, clear sky. *Beautiful*.

"Why should I be ashamed, exactly?"

"Because you take advantage of people."

"I most certainly do not," he said, his shoulders stiffening in rising annoyance. "I would never dream of forcing someone to do anything he or she hadn't agreed to."

"Agreed to. Right. Like anybody agrees to get wiped out."

Wiped out? He wasn't familiar with that expression. But before he could ask her about it, she jabbed an index finger in his direction. "How do you people live with yourselves?"

"We people?" He was about to explain that royals rarely lived by themselves, that there were lots of people in the palaces and castles. His was a large family; though Philip was an only child, he had many cousins and other relations.

But he remembered at the last moment that he was supposed to be a poor student from another land—he'd even picked one out of an atlas—and shook his head sadly. "Only with great difficulty."

"No kidding. I don't know how you can sleep at night."

"I sleep very well," he told her, wondering how she slept. And where she slept. And who she slept with.

Oh yes, he wanted very much to know that. Especially because, despite the fact that she was scolding him for some reason, and that her accusations had begun to annoy him, he couldn't deny that he quite adored the passion in her eyes and the way her glorious lips pursed when she was angry.

"I don't see how, considering the way you people prey on naive, brainless twenty-one-year-olds."

"Brainless?" he asked, unaccustomed to the slang here. He didn't imagine she meant that literally, but one never knew. There had been, of course, that straw man in his world.

"Yeah. He's not smart enough to deal with the likes of you and your boss."

"I don't have a boss."

"Strictly contract work, huh?"

More confusing by the moment. But it seemed safe to simply agree. "I suppose you could say that."

"That's disgusting."

Well, *that* had been the wrong answer. But Philip didn't persist, nor did he question her. In honesty, he was barely paying attention anymore to the strange things she said. He was focused only on the strength in her voice, the stiffness in her posture, the belligerence of her words. And the way all those things combined to make her one dazzlingly exciting female.

He stepped closer, drawn to the fire in her, the fervency in her tone—the disrespect, the near dislike—shocking and attracting him all at once. Very rarely had a woman spoken to him in such a manner. In fact, he could recall only one, a feisty historian he'd met a few months before. This woman reminded him of her in some ways. She had...spirit.

His tread quiet on the floor, courtesy of his new, rubber-soled shoes—supposedly a staple of college students—Philip continued to move toward her. He heard her tiny gasp and knew she was alarmed. But he also saw the way her lips parted, her small tongue slipping out to moisten them. Her pulse fluttered in her throat as her breathing quickened, and the warm pink color in her cheeks deepened to crimson the closer he came.

So, the fiery stranger was not immune to him, as much as she might wish otherwise.

"Don't come any closer," she ordered, though her voice quavered. She reached down and picked up the spoon she'd dropped, leaving a thin trail of gooey, liquid chocolate on the countertop. Ignoring that, she waved the spoon at him threateningly, sending a few tiny droplets his way. One landed on his shirt, another on his lower lip.

Philip had always had a weakness for chocolate. As a child, he'd often sneaked into the kitchens and filched desserts, which his father had said was unbecoming of a prince. There was just something decadent about chocolate, something forbidden, dark, slick and luscious. It appealed to all his senses.

He licked his mouth, tasting this concoction, which was like nothing he'd ever experienced. It wasn't as sweet or milky as he was used to. It was dark and strong, with enough sweetness to soothe the palate, and the tiniest bite of peppery spice to arouse the senses. He groaned with pleasure as he swallowed.

"By the gods, that's incredible."

"Huh?" She sounded thoroughly confused.

Philip didn't answer. Instead, he reached out and clasped her wrist. As if stunned, she didn't protest. He drew the hand—and the spoon she held—closer, until he could flick out his tongue and taste the dark, gooey substance that drenched it.

The woman—this strange, beautiful, fiery woman—watched him raptly. As if she'd never seen a man take such pleasure in eating.

Philip enjoyed indulging his senses, and he wasn't sure which delighted him more right now—tasting the decadence gliding down his throat or watching the woman stare in fascination as he did so. "This is remarkable," he said as he delicately licked off every drop. "Did you make it?"

"I'm melting it for a recipe. You…like to eat chocolate?"

"I like to eat *your* chocolate."

She coughed into her fist, then yanked her hand away. Seeing the way her eyes had dropped to his mouth, and she'd pressed her other hand into her middle, as if she needed to grab on to something, he suspected he knew why.

"That was suggestive, wasn't it?" he asked, hearing the unintentional purr in his tone. Something about the eroticism of licking his favorite delicacy off a spoon held in the hand of a strange and seductive woman had sent warm waves of sexual pleasure through him. They'd obviously translated to her.

"Very."

"Should I apologize?"

"Only if you're sincere."

He didn't apologize. Because though he'd only been telling the truth about how much he enjoyed her tasty concoction, he couldn't deny that he liked the idea of tasting *her,* as well.

Silence descended. She was waiting for the words—sincere or not—but he didn't speak. As her breathing became more audible, the electric spark between them intensified, until it seemed like a tangible thing. It enveloped them, shifted back and forth between them, drawing him to her as if with magnetic force.

He knew things were different in this world. In some ways more free, in others more rigid. He also knew he had no right to take anything this woman hadn't freely offered, in any world.

She might not have said it aloud, but her eyes were offering. Her lips were offering. Her body was offering, considering the way she swayed toward him as if against her will.

So he took.

Without a word, he slid his hands into her thick hair, sending glossy strands tumbling, and dragged her to him for a deep, hungry, chocolate-flavored kiss.

2

He was kissing her.

Claire registered that much, accepted the fact that a complete stranger—one who should be in the dictionary defining tall, dark and handsome—had his lips on hers and was, oh, God, plunging his warm, delicious tongue into her mouth.

Then reality left. Just walked out the door, taking a huge chunk of her common sense with it.

She responded. Heaven help her, everything else just faded away and she could focus only on the strength of his magnificent body pressed against hers, and the taste of his mouth.

Chocolate had always been her favorite flavor, but she had never realized that it was missing something, some vital, intrinsic ingredient. Not until now, when she finally got to taste decadent melted Godiva spiced with powerful, devouring man.

She dropped the spoon, hearing it clatter to the floor, as if from a very far distance. Lifting her hands, she put them on his shoulders, while a voice inside screamed at her to push him away. But those traitorous things at the ends of her arms clung to him instead, her fingers digging into the thick muscles as she held tight and kissed him back.

She liked kissing. She loved it, actually. And considering

she'd been single for more than a year, she'd missed the intimacy. Especially because this…well, this went beyond anything she'd ever experienced.

Their tongues twirled together, hot and hungry. Time and place fell away and there became nothing but this moment, this man, this kiss. They shared each breath, shared the same space as their bodies melded, her hands going around his neck, one of his dropping to the small of her back to pull her hard against his groin.

She gasped, feeling the rigid erection pressed against her. Part of her leaped for joy, wanting it—wanting that. But the smart, rational Claire, who'd been gagged and shoved in a mental closet for the last ninety seconds, finally came barreling out and screamed *Stop!*

"No," she exclaimed, pulling her mouth away. Sanity required her to also take a full step back, ignoring the look of disappointment that appeared on his oh-so-handsome face. That not being far enough, she hopped back another step, colliding with the counter and wincing in pain.

"Are you all right?" he asked, his brow furrowed in concern as he reached for her.

"I'm fine." She shoved his hand back and ducked away from him, darting around the counter to watch him from the relative safety of the other side.

Safety? Hell, three feet wasn't a safe distance, not from a man this incredibly alluring.

And dangerous. Don't forget dangerous. He's a bad guy, remember? A thug sent here to rough up your kid brother!

Okay, so sometimes even she felt as if Freddy needed a slap upside the head. But no way was she going to let some dude crack his—er, no way would she let the Nutcracker do his thing.

It seemed not only impossible but actually criminal that someone this smooth and sexy should be a criminal. Villains were supposed to be brawny and beastly, like something out of a Disney cartoon, complete with broken noses, crooked or missing teeth, bulging foreheads and tree-trunk-size necks.

Uh-uh. Not this guy.

While he was very tall, with wide shoulders and a broad, rock-hard chest that she could almost still feel pressed against her sensitized body, he wasn't at all beefy or brawny. He instead looked and felt like the perfect man should. Powerful but lean, muscular but elegant, somehow. He moved almost gracefully, not a lumbering beast, more a prowling predator.

She'd definitely felt stalked as he'd moved close enough to…sample her chocolate.

But it wasn't just his body that had sucked her brain cells dry and let her kiss a complete stranger. There was also his face. Oh, Lord, that face. He was perfect, been sculpted from marble… His skin was a bit dark, as if he had just come from someplace sunny, or was of Mediterranean—Italian?— descent. The fineness of his brow was accentuated by the widow's peak that pierced it. His cheekbones were high and autocratic, his cheeks lean, his nose straight and proud, that jaw strong, with a delicious-looking cleft at the bottom. His thick hair was jet-black, short, but wavy and incredibly finger-tempting. And his eyes—those almost intrusive, assessing, deep-set and heavily lashed eyes—were dark brown…like her favorite semisweet confections.

All that and a chocaholic. The man was simply divine.

Ding-ding-ding, hello in there? He wants to hurt your brother. Remember?

She would never let him get close to Freddy. Claire had promised their mother on her deathbed that she would look out for her baby brother. Allowing him to be…de-testicled wouldn't just be neglecting her responsibilities, it would be unforgivable.

"*Now* should I offer my apologies?" the sexy stranger

asked, his dark eyes gleaming in the soft glow of the overhead lights. Both amusement and awareness shone in those depths, also revealed by the slight uptilting of his soft, sensuous mouth.

I kissed that mouth? I was held by this man?

Impossible. Those kinds of wild, romantic moments happened to other women. To helpless, small, delicate, beautiful women. Not to blunt, responsible, down-to-earth Amazons like Claire Hoffman.

"Only if you're sincere," she mumbled, swallowing.

Considering her words were the volume of a mouse's squeak, she couldn't say there was much chance she'd get an apology.

"Let me rephrase that. Do I have anything to apologize for?"

Did he? He hadn't exactly forced her. Yeah, he'd started the kiss, but he hadn't grabbed her, pushed her up against the refrigerator and ripped her clothes off.

Oh, wow.

Stop, stop, stop!

Angry at her traitorous body, which demanded he do anything *but* apologize, she dodged the question altogether. "Look, I'm not letting you touch Freddy. Kissing me isn't going to work any more than threatening me would have."

He flinched, as if slapped, and for the first time since he'd entered the kitchen, he looked angry. "Threatening you? I would never threaten a woman."

How noble. Hence the name? No nuts, no worries? "So you save your threats for young, inexperienced fools like my brother?"

"Your brother?" That fine brow went up and he tilted his handsome head in confusion. "Mr. Hoffman?"

"Yes. Freddy's my brother. And if you think I'm going to let you hurt him, you've got another think coming."

"Shouldn't that be another *thought* coming?"

She growled. "What are you, the freaking grammar police?"

"I'm not from this area, and I am not sure I understand all your colloquialisms."

"Where do you come from?" she asked, though she cursed herself for doing so. She had no interest in the man, and this conversation was beyond confusing.

"The land of Barcelona," he declared with a decisive nod.

"Uh…Spain? You sure don't sound Spanish."

He waved a hand. "I am well traveled…but, um, but also poor. A student making my way around the world."

Huh. That was surprising. The guy oozed confidence and self-reliance, looking more like a ship's captain or a…a sheik—that was it, some oil-rich gazillionaire. Yes, his clothes were casual, and didn't appear terribly expensive, but he wore them like somebody who had money.

He had the leanest waist and hips, most attractive male butt and strong legs…at least, as far as she could tell. And considering she'd been pressed up against him five minutes ago, she could tell a lot. So, really, anything would look phenomenal on the man.

Or off the man.

She swallowed hard, trying to focus. "So tell me, *student,* what are you learning from your boss, the bookie? How to swindle people? How to…crack nuts?"

"You keep talking about this nut cracking. I'm afraid I don't understand."

There was no disguising the confusion in his voice. For the first time, a hint of uncertainty entered Claire's mind.

She'd turned around and found a big, strong, dark and mysterious stranger in the shop kitchen, asking for Freddy. Her mind had immediately connected him with the deadly man her brother had warned her about a few days ago.

But what if he wasn't who she thought he was? What if she'd mistaken him for a mobster, when he was just… Just what? Looking for directions to the Statue of Liberty by slipping in the back door of a closed candy shop on a Sunday evening?

Something didn't add up. But she had to know for sure.

"Who, exactly, are you?"

"I'm Philip." He extended his hand. "Philip…Smith."

She eyed it as if it were poisonous. Not because she didn't want to touch him, to feel his hand in hers and assess its strength, and imagine how it might feel rubbing against parts of her body. But rather, because she did.

Finally, though, realizing he wasn't going to drop his arm until she shook, she reached out and grasped his fingers with hers, squeezing lightly, pumping once and yanking away.

No matter how quickly she moved, it wasn't fast enough. She was still left with curiosity about other squeezing and pumping. Lots of squeezing and pumping.

Pull your head out of his pants. It had obviously been too long since she'd gotten laid if she was thinking about sex with a guy who might or might not be here to neuter her brother.

The stranger was watching her closely, his eyebrows raised expectantly, and she finally remembered he'd offered her his name.

"I'm Claire Hoffman," she mumbled.

"Claire. I'm pleased to make your acquaintance."

Was he for real? Would a mob enforcer really talk like that?

"And if you run the delightful shop, in which I purchased some festive holiday candies yesterday, it appears I am your upstairs neighbor."

"Wha-a-a…?"

Good thing she was leaning against the counter, not only because her legs suddenly felt weak, but because there would be something to catch her plummeting jaw as it collapsed downward. She stared at the man, putting the pieces together, remembering how Freddy had cajoled her to rent the up-stairs apartments to get him his gambling money. They hadn't talked about it since; she'd been busy decorating the shop and restocking specific seasonal goodies. Could he—would he—have done it behind her back? Would even weak, spoiled Freddy do something so rotten?

You didn't. Oh, God, tell me you didn't.

But she knew he had. Freddy had already had this plan in mind, or perhaps even in motion, when he'd come to her about the money the other day. Then when he'd asked her to meet him at his place to talk some more yesterday, he'd stood her up. She'd had to get her part-timer to cover the store on a busy Saturday afternoon, and Freddy hadn't even been there.

Because he was here, renting those apartments?

Oh, that sneaky bastard.

"Now tell me," Philip ordered, "who did you think I was when I first came in? And why did the thought of that person being here frighten you?"

"I wasn't frightened."

"I think you were," he said, those dark eyes piercing, de-manding she reveal the truth.

"I thought it might be somebody looking for my brother."

"Someone who wanted to hurt your brother?" The man's tone said he wouldn't accept anything less than pure honesty. "Someone who'd threatened him?"

"Maybe."

Her visitor's jaw clenched; she could see the flexing of his muscles.

"Would this person hurt *you* to get at your brother?"

She shifted her gaze, not knowing what Freddy's cohorts were capable of.

Philip's whole body seemed to grow bigger, harder—more threatening—as he leaned closer. "I walked right in. Why are you working here alone at night? Your brother should be here protecting you!"

Laughter burst from her mouth at the very idea. "Freddy couldn't protect his graham crackers from the other kids in day care."

"He doesn't sound like much of a man."

"He's only twenty-one," she said, not even sure why she was making excuses for her sibling. "And I've sort of had to finish raising him since our mother died."

Or, well, all his life. But who was counting?

"At twenty-one you're a man," Philip insisted, "in any land. It's wrong that he put you in such a position." Her visitor cast a quick, malevolent glance toward the door. "Don't worry, if this dangerous person comes looking for him now, I'll take care of it. You don't have to worry anymore. You're no longer alone."

Right. No longer alone. Because he freaking lived upstairs! How she'd let herself be distracted from that, she had no idea.

Then she realized it was probably because it had been such a long time since anyone had acted protectively toward her. Maybe it was a little overbearing, and maybe he did sound like a caveman, but something about the idea of this hot, sexy man wanting to protect her seemed incredibly exciting.

But he wouldn't be around to make good. He couldn't possibly. Because there was no way she could let him stay. He was going to have to leave her life just as quickly as he'd come into it.

Why that thought sent a sharp stab of regret rushing through her, she couldn't say. It made no sense; she barely knew him. But there was no other choice.

Swallowing and taking a deep breath, she spoke, "You know what? I think we have some talking to do. So how about you sit down and we figure out exactly what's going on here."

Except she knew what was going on.

She'd been scammed by her own brother. And now she had to figure out how to get rid of her unwanted upstairs neighbor.

THOUGH IT TOOK SOME cursing, mumbling, hair twisting and chocolate eating—everything other than the chocolate part coming from *her,* the beautiful woman he still tasted on his lips—Philip had finally figured out what had happened. Claire Hoffman owned the building in which he sat. She had not authorized her wastrel brother to rent out any of the upstairs units, and was both furious and fearful. Furious at the position her sibling had put her in, and fearful of how Philip would react to her attempts to back out of the deal.

Well, that wasn't going to happen. Her brother might not have had the legal right to offer Philip and his entourage the dwellings, but he had accepted money for them and scrawled a signature on a contract, one his sister carefully examined when Philip withdrew it from his pocket. And while he might not be accustomed to all the ways of this world, he knew a few things, including a bit about the law.

She could make him leave. But he could then go to the authorities and charge her brother with fraud or theft.

The way she stumbled over her words and wouldn't meet Philip's eye said she knew it. But she wasn't ready to give up.

"So you see," she said, twisting her hands in front of her on the broad counter, "I couldn't possibly let you and your two friends stay in those apartments. They're really not in any condition to be lived in."

"They are acceptable to me."

"You don't understand. I *can't* let you stay."

Maybe not. Maybe, in fact, Philip didn't really need to stay. He could certainly afford to find another place to live. It might not be quite as perfect for his plan to pose as a poor man, while also being able to stay in the heart of the most exciting city in this world, but it could be done.

He wasn't going to do it, however.

Because of her.

First, because there was no way on Elatyria he was leaving this woman alone to deal with the dangerous criminal she'd thought him to be. He suspected her brother owed someone money and would use the cash Philip had given him to pay off the debt. But what if he hadn't? What if he'd pocketed it and left the city, leaving his sister to deal with his mess—and his creditors?

Oh, no. Philip wasn't leaving her unprotected, not by any means, whether she liked it or not. If he, Shelby and Teeny had to take shifts guarding the door to her shop—or the one that led to her apartment—that's what they'd do.

Aside from wishing to protect her, he simply wanted to know more about this woman, Claire Hoffman, who was calling to him, drawing him like no one ever had. Perhaps it was because she was talking in circles, telling tales of terror—as if a few bugs or sagging floors mattered—to make him leave. Perhaps because of the way she'd tasted and felt in his arms. Perhaps because she was trying so desperately to pretend she hadn't been every bit as affected by that warm, hungry kiss as he had.

Whatever the reason, he had found her, he'd kissed her, and he still wanted her. So he wasn't going anywhere.

"I'm afraid I can't simply move back out," he told her when she stopped for breath. "Unless, of course, you can return all of the money I gave your brother." He was certain she couldn't.

She nibbled her lip. "Uh, how much was that, exactly?"

"Fifteen thousand American dollars."

She coughed so hard she fell off her stool. Fortunately, Philip had quick reflexes and dived off his own to grab her before she could hit the floor. He landed on his knees, catching her in his arms and yanking her protectively against his body.

Raspy breaths escaped her mouth and she looked at him, blinking rapidly. He could feel the wild thudding of her heart against his chest, and wondered whether she was alarmed by her near miss…or by his nearness.

"Thank you," she whispered.

"You are most welcome."

They stayed that way for a moment, staring at each other, and Philip tried very hard to count the number of blue flecks in her green eyes—or green flecks in her blue ones—before finally remembering he should probably let her up.

Moving slowly, carefully, to make sure she didn't slip— either to the floor, or closer against any of his body parts that were reacting mightily to having her in his arms again—he gently set her down, then rose to his feet and pulled her up, as well.

"I take it that's more than you can pay back?" he murmured.

"Definitely more." She swallowed visibly. "He actually charged you fifteen thousand dollars for those apartments?"

"Yes, five thousand per month for each unit, plus another five as a security deposit."

She shook her head. "Yeah, sure. Because there's so much valuable stuff that could be damaged or broken."

Sarcasm was common in his world, too, but he quite liked how she did it.

"Fifteen thousand dollars," she repeated to herself.

"That was almost all the money I had. The, uh, the people in my village back home took up a collection to send me here," he said quickly, realizing this was quite a lot of money.

She scrunched her brow. "Isn't Barcelona a big city?"

A misfire. Damnation, he should have studied his backstory more. Aware that the best way to avoid answering an uncomfortable question was to shrug it off, he shrugged. "It is therefore more than I can afford to lose," he told her, which wasn't exactly true, but wasn't totally a lie.

The amount was nothing overall, but in terms of his presence here in New York, it was important. He had brought only a certain amount of cash from the vault at home—his father always keeping a supply of various currencies on hand for traveling expenses—and had to make it last. Philip couldn't start all over with another housing situation without coming perilously close to the limit of his funds. That would leave him having to sell something—possibly one of Shelby's bejeweled rings, which Philip would of course replace. But it would hardly be worth the man's whining.

"I can't afford that," she said, sounding on the verge of tears.

He hated that her brother had done this to her, and thought for a moment of telling her he'd reconsidered and would leave. The money truly meant nothing to him.

But she might. And he simply couldn't walk away without knowing for sure.

"You don't have to," he told her, reaching out and taking her hand in his. A strong hand, but still soft, pretty.

She tensed for a moment, staring at their fingers twined together on the counter, then relaxed.

"So it is settled," he said, sure she'd begun to accept the inevitability of it. "We will stay."

"You can't seriously want to."

"Of course we want to."

"The place is a dump!"

"A…"

"It's a wreck. A mess. A ruin."

"I am aware it's not in the best condition. It needs a bit of work, but I'm sure my…friends and I can make do."

"You almost sound as if you *like* the idea of having to stay here."

"I do."

"Why? I mean, there are better locations, and definitely better buildings."

He couldn't tell her the truth, couldn't possibly admit that he was staying because of her. Because she was in danger. Because she'd fought him and confronted him and disliked him—and yet still kissed him as if she needed his breath to survive. Because she was, right now, rubbing the soft pad of her thumb against his, sending frissons of sensation through him as he imagined all the other ways, other places, he wanted her touch.

So he settled for replying, "It's where I need to be, and you can't pay me back, so I'm making the best of it."

She blinked rapidly, nibbled her lip and pulled her hand away to clench it with her other one. Finally, as if not quite believing she was saying it, she agreed.

"All right, then. If you're completely sure, I guess you've got yourself a place to live for the month. But just until the New Year."

Actually, he didn't have quite that much time. He'd lost days in travel, and would on the way home, too. So he had only a little over three weeks before he'd have to start heading back to Elatyria. Less than one month of freedom before his responsibilities would take over his life.

Not much time to find the woman of his dreams, one he could love for the rest of his days.

Or, in case he'd already found her, not much time to make her fall in love with him in return.

3

ALTHOUGH PHILIP WAS certain Claire was the only woman he wanted to get to know, his two compatriots insisted he follow his original plan to meet as many as possible before pursuing anyone. He'd had to keep an open mind and at least allow the possibility that he'd meet someone else who interested him more.

So, despite wanting to do nothing but find reasons to bump into the lady, which he did a few times—or better yet, find reasons to kiss her again—he had to leave the apartment and get out and about in New York. He visited museums, rode the subway, consumed horrible coffee in dingy cafés and excellent Scotch in swanky restaurants. He was flirted with, propositioned, and even argued over by two women at a club—yet his heart didn't so much as skip a beat for any other female he set eyes on. Only *her*.

Whenever he wasn't out fulfilling his obligations to his kingdom and his family, he was at the apartment, fulfilling his vow to protect Claire. She didn't know the Elatyrians were on guard. It seemed American women were touchy about being protected by a man.

Philip kept watch from the stairs, or the back alley, or from across the street. Shelby had complained incessantly, especially about the cold, but Teeny was happy to help, since being a bodyguard was his job and his favorite thing to do. He would love for something to happen so he could crush someone, and Philip had had to physically drag him away from a taxi driver who'd paused in front of Claire's shop for too long.

After a few days, Philip began to relax his guard, feeling fairly confident they hadn't overlooked any scurrilous characters lurking around, and he released his friends from their duty. But he didn't release himself. He kept watching, not only because it was still possible she could be in danger, but because he'd rather stay here, getting to know her moment by stolen moment, than exchange a word with anyone else.

Guarding her had given him the chance to see her in so many guises. Claire was always smiling and friendly toward her customers, patient with her annoyingly perky clerk. She looked happy when hanging colorful holiday decorations in the window, and he'd heard her humming Christmas tunes when closing up at night. She always bent down to eye level when a child entered the shop and usually slipped the little ones a free chocolate if their parents approved.

Every morning, after the early rush and before the lunchhour one, she would sit at the same small table in the front window. She'd slowly sip a cup of coffee, staring out at the world with a dreamy expression on her face, as if for those few minutes she was allowing herself to let go of her responsibilities and thinking only lovely thoughts.

He liked those moments especially. Claire looked young and fragile and almost carefree, when usually she was so strong and hardworking. But always beautiful.

Sometimes, though, she looked utterly weary. Like right now.

Philip stood at the top of the staircase, watching from the shadows. Though not on constant vigil, he did like to keep an eye out after she closed up, wanting to be there when she made the short walk down the darkened hall from her store to her small apartment. Since she usually kept the back door to the building unlocked during the day for deliveries, he was always tense about these transition times and wanted to make sure she got there safely.

Tonight, she looked exhausted, having worked a long, ten-hour shift by herself. Her eyes were shadowed, her face pale. She hadn't even finished locking the shop door behind her before she was reaching up to tug at the clips in her bun, letting the thick mass of dark hair tumble down over her shoulders. It fell in a sea of curls to midway down her back, luscious and inviting, like the richest chocolate she sold.

Philip made a small sound of approval, not even realizing he'd done it until she jerked her head and peered up into the shadows, her eyes wide, a little frightened.

"Pardon me, I didn't mean to startle you," he said, walking down the stairs toward her.

"Oh, it's you," she replied, her voice holding a tremor. He wondered if she'd had a few sleepless nights, waiting for her brother's unsavory friends to pay a visit. "What are you doing?"

Philip lifted a bag of rubbish that he'd brought along in case they bumped into one another. "Just taking this out."

"Okay." She lifted a hand, self-consciously smoothing her hair, as if uncomfortable about having taken it down.

"It's beautiful," he told her sincerely, though he wished the hallway wasn't so shadowy, so he could see all the variations of color. What he'd originally thought was simply a dark, rich brown appeared to have lighter streaks, but he couldn't be sure. "Keeping it up and hidden away is criminal."

There was a brief hesitation while she stared at him, as if unsure how to respond. He sensed she was unused to compliments. Which told him men here were not only blind but stupid.

Finally, she chuckled softly. "Tell that to a customer who finds a long strand of hair in his candy. Eww."

Philip conceded the point. "When you are not working, then." Reaching out, he smoothed an errant strand, fingering its softness, then tucked it behind her ear.

She sucked in a breath. Philip dropped his hand. The air in the cramped hallway seemed to grow hotter by the second as awareness and tension flowed between them.

He knew what attraction felt like, knew the lure of sexual heat, and right now it was building like a huge, tangible presence between them.

"So, are you settling in okay? I've heard you guys moving around a lot, but haven't seen much of you over the past few days. I've never even met your friends."

Her voice held the tiniest hint of wistfulness. A less confident man might not have heard it, or might have misinterpreted, but Philip recognized it.

He mentally kicked himself. After the kiss they'd shared, she had to have been wondering if he had romantic intentions toward her. In fulfilling his obligations—continuing his bride hunt—for the past four days, he'd ignored the one woman he actually wanted.

Well, that was something he intended to remedy. Very soon.

"We're fine," he assured her. "We've just been getting our living quarters established. There is a lot to do."

She sighed and ran a hand through her thick hair. "I know. I'm sorry. I should have come up and offered to clean—"

"Don't be ridiculous. You're not a maidservant."

"No, but I could have at least made sure there were no dead bugs all over the floor."

"There aren't." A tiny grin lifted the corners of his mouth. "Anymore."

"Gross," she said with a reluctant laugh. "I suck at this landlady thing."

"As I recall, it wasn't a job you chose."

"True."

"Speaking of which, have you heard from your brother?"

Her lips tightened. "Not a single word."

Not surprising. The cheerful young man hadn't looked like the type who would enjoy being confronted by anyone, especially an angry sister. "I'm sure he's all right."

She growled. "He won't be after I feed him a batch of fudge with a laxative icing."

Philip didn't know exactly what she meant, but got the feeling it didn't bode well for Freddy. "Poisoning your sibling isn't very nice," he said, while privately conceding her brother likely deserved it.

"He won't die," she insisted.

He laughed softly. "Bloodthirsty, are you? I didn't think you capable of murder, Claire."

"You should have seen me after you left Sunday night."

He had seen her. Every time he closed his eyes.

She leaned against the hallway wall. "So, have you gotten out at all to see New York?"

"A bit."

He told her of his adventures with the subway, hearing her chuckle as he admitted he'd ridden the thing for four hours straight one day, being unsure where to get off. She gave him a few tips, talked about her own favorite things to do in the city…and gave him an idea for his next move.

Now wasn't a good time. She looked exhausted, having worked alone all day. Plus he had some plans to make. But very soon, he would, as they said here, take his best shot.

"I should let you get inside," he told her when he saw her struggling to hide a yawn. "You look most weary."

"You can say that again. Making ten dozen truffles really shouldn't be such backbreaking work."

The days to come would be better; she wouldn't have to work so hard. He'd make sure of it, even if he had to send Shelby to sell sweets in the store and set Teeny to baking in the kitchen, so Claire was able to take a break now and then. Picturing such a thing, he smiled.

"What?"

"I'm just imagining my…friend Teeny working in your kitchen, making delicate chocolates. 'Tis not a pretty picture."

"Bull-in-the-china-shop sort?"

"More like a mastodon."

She chuckled, as if visualizing it. "I'm afraid I can't give him a job right now, anyway. I can barely make payroll for my salesclerk, who I can afford only four days a week."

Hmm. How much, he wondered, would a kitchen assistant require? And could the salesclerk be persuaded to work a few more hours for money slipped to her on the side?

"Well, I should go in," Claire said.

"Yes, of course. Good night," he told her, resisting the urge to touch her again.

But he would, very soon. He just had a few things to work out. In the meantime, he would get to know her, be someone she could rely on. He would befriend her, with courtesy and politeness. And see what happened.

"Good night, Philip."

Her smile was gentle, sweet, and his heart clenched as she nodded and walked to her door. After she unlocked it and let herself inside, he listened for the click of the bolt. Once he was sure she was safely locked in, he made his way back upstairs, but didn't go into his cold, lonely apartment just yet. Instead, he stood on the landing for several long minutes, thinking about that smile, that laugh, that naughty gleam in her eye. Thinking about that hair. About sinking his hands into it and feeling it brush against his bare skin...his chest, his throat, his stomach.

That was when he acknowledged that he'd wasted enough time looking for someone else. The only woman he wanted lived right downstairs from him. He could walk around for days, find ways to be introduced to a hundred more single woman and still not be drawn to anyone the way he was to Claire Hoffman.

And so as soon as he could arrange it, his courtship of her would begin in earnest.

CLAIRE HAD BEEN TELLING herself for several days that she didn't mind that her handsome tenant hadn't sought her out in private after that first night. Yes, he'd kissed her. Yes, he'd rocked her world in the process. Yes, he'd left her dazed, confused and dreaming fantastic dreams every night since. But he hadn't promised anything.

Maybe in Spain, deep tongue kisses meant "Nice to meet you."

After she'd finally had another conversation with him, outside her apartment Thursday night, however, she was forced to admit the truth to herself. She'd been bothered that he hadn't pursued her. Seriously bothered. She was attracted to the man in a way she'd never been attracted to anyone. She just didn't know what she was going to do about it.

As ridiculous as it seemed, she tried to intentionally run into him again throughout the next few days. She lingered in the hallway during her breaks. She hovered at the bottom of the stairs, or at the entrance to the building a few times. She certainly heard noises from upstairs, or sometimes from the hallway, when they were hauling in furniture that looked like it had come from the dump or the junk store.

And her plan worked; she did see him and talk to him. But never with the intimacy of the night they'd met, or the time he'd been taking out the trash. Now when they bumped into each other Philip was polite and courteous, insisting on opening doors for her, and once helping her move a stack of boxes to the stockroom. She tried not to notice the way his shirt pulled tight against his arms and shoulders when he moved. But that would be like trying not to notice a tsunami roaring up the Hudson.

Beyond that, though, they'd been nothing but cordial. Like real neighbors. Mr. Tall, Dark and Sexy was the perfect tenant—which was a good thing, right?

Wrong. Because she felt she was missing out on something every time he was cordial, when she wanted him to be flirtatious. Every time he held the door, when she wanted him to hold *her.*

Now, she probably wouldn't even have that much. Christmas was exactly two weeks away, and she would be incredibly busy with the store. Though, she conceded, not as busy as she'd feared. To her surprise—and delight—an older lady who'd once owned a candy shop and was looking for something to do now that she'd been widowed, had come in looking for a job on Saturday, and had gone right to work. Mrs. West had insisted on working for a low salary to "get back in the game" as she called it, and had quickly become indispensable. Not only was she wonderful in the kitchen, she had a sharp mind for business and had made several great suggestions.

What a godsend. And not only that, Jean, her part-time salesperson, had said she needed a few more hours, and had agreed to let Claire pay her every two weeks instead of weekly so it would be easier for her to make payroll. Businesswise, things were going well.

Personally? Not so much.

It wasn't just Philip. Claire also hadn't seen or spoken with her idiot, soon-to-be-seriously-smacked-if-she-had-anything-to-say-about-it brother. Freddy hadn't been coming around, nor had he returned any of her dozen messages. Probably because he knew she would, A) want to do violence on his person; and B) demand that he give her the five thousand dollars he'd scammed off Philip so she could pay back the man's security deposit when he moved out.

She had no idea how she was going to do that, and found herself half hoping they'd decide to stay another month so she could tell him he didn't have to pay, that she'd take the rent out of the deposit. Then she could write it off and call it even. Even if they stayed, that wouldn't allow her to recoup the money she'd had to pay to get the utilities turned on upstairs, but it was better than trying to come up with five "large."

That, she promised herself, was the *only* reason she wanted Philip Smith to stick around. It had nothing to do with his looks or his smooth voice, his sexy smile, or, oh, God, that incredible kiss.

"Are you okay?" asked Jeannie, who, like Claire, had been working like a madwoman during the late afternoon rush on Tuesday. Word was spreading about I Want Candy and people were constantly calling or coming in to place orders for specialized holiday gifts. Claire had gone through so much red and green icing, she wished she owned stock in Dixie Kane sugar. "You're so quiet."

"I'm fine, just thinking," Claire admitted. "I've barely had time to do that lately."

She'd looked at the clock during a lull that afternoon, and then three hours had passed in a blur of customers and phone calls. It was nearly six now, almost closing time and already dark out, if Midtown Manhattan could ever be called dark. Especially at this time of year, with all the twinkling lights and holiday decorations brightening even the gloomiest of nights.

"Hey, I finally met one of the new guys."

"New guys?"

"One of the dudes from upstairs. Talk about a hottie."

Claire immediately turned and busied herself filing some cleared order forms. "Oh?"

"He's very gentlemanly, too. Treated me like I was all highbrow and stuff."

Jeannie cracked her gum. *So highbrow.*

Claire had already talked to her about that habit, among others, but the young woman, while a hard worker, and smart, sometimes seemed to have the attention span of a three-year-old on Pixy Stix. Which was a good thing when it came to her energy level and enthusiasm, but a bad one about stuff like follow-through.

"Yes, I suppose."

"Is he single?" Jeannie asked.

Claire's hand tightened on the top receipt and she found herself crumpling it, then forced her fingers to relax. "I have no idea."

If not, he's got some explaining to do about that kiss.

"I mean, I assume he is, since it's just guys up there. Unless they're... You don't think they're gay, do you?"

She barked a laugh. "Definitely not."

"Yeah, didn't think so. He's supergentlemanly and all, but he didn't set off my gaydar."

What a joke. The man's testosterone had testosterone. He was utterly male, masculine, confidently sexual, sensual and dangerous as hell to any woman who was the least bit susceptible to dark, mysterious strangers.

Which Claire wasn't. Right?

"Oh, wow, there he is now," Jeannie said, pointing toward the front of the shop.

Her heart lurching, Claire glanced at the door and saw a dark-haired man entering. But it wasn't the one who made her pulse race and her underwear dampen.

"Hey, handsome," said Jeannie with a simper.

"Good evening," the stranger replied, his voice slightly

accented, as Philip's was. He was also similarly featured, and good-looking, but something about the way his chin and nose were held higher than absolutely necessary told Claire he wasn't much like the man she'd met in her kitchen.

Still, better this man—who didn't confuse and attract her—than his friend—who did.

Claire had just breathed a sigh of relief that she wasn't going to come face-to-face with the guy she couldn't stop thinking about when the door swung open again, sending in a blast of cold air and hot man.

Oh, boy, here we go.

It was him. Big, strong, so unbelievably handsome, his hair windswept, his mouth curved in a smile that could stop traffic.

Panty-dampening time. Damn it all.

She turned and began shoveling chocolates molded into wreath, bell and Santa shapes from one tray to another. Then she put them back. Busy hands made a clean mind, or something like that. Actually, all her busy hands made was smeary chocolate.

"Hello, Claire," he said, his voice smooth, silky. Close.

She spun around, to find him standing directly in front of her on the other side of the counter. "Uh, hi. How's it going?"

"How is what going?"

She took a deep breath and tried again, wondering why this guy so easily flustered her. She'd never had trouble talking to a man before, but Philip left her unsure of herself and a little dizzy.

"How are you doing? Is everything all right upstairs?"

He nodded once. "All is well. Quite comfortable, though I did have to bring someone in to fix the heating apparatus."

Oh, great. Something else she owed him for.

"Shelby is most happy that it is working now."

"How could anyone survive this climate without it?" called

Philip's companion—Shelby?—obviously overhearing. Then he went back to flirting with Jeannie, whose attention appeared to have drifted from her original hottie to the inferno who was now speaking to Claire. She was staring back and forth between them like a kid in a...well, whatever.

"Sorry about that," Claire said. "If you give me the receipt for the service call, I'll pay you back."

"No need, it was quite inexpensive. And I wasn't truly bothered by the cold, though we do come from a warm climate," Philip said, that purr in his voice making her think of all kinds of warm, sweaty things.

"Oh. Well, I can see how that would be different. It does get pretty cold here," she mumbled.

Reduced to talking about the weather? Was this really the best she could do? Her late mother, once a noted femme fatale, would be rolling over in her grave.

Her mom had given up on Claire having any grace or feminine wiles by the time she was ten and hit five-eight. Claire had been all lanky build, clumsy feet, gangly arms and legs. Nothing like her petite, delicate mother, the ballerina, who'd been adored by men all over the country once upon a time. That was when Claire had finally been allowed to quit ballet lessons—which she'd loathed. She'd then focused on the one thing she'd loved to do since she'd been old enough to beg her grandmother to let her help in the kitchen: bake.

"And you? You are well?" her tenant asked.

"I'm fine."

"There have been no...incidents?"

"Incidents?"

"No strangers bothering you?"

Realizing what he was talking about, she shook her head. "No. I don't think there's anything to worry about anymore."

"Not even this Mr. Nutcracker?"

Claire chuckled under her breath as she remembered she'd

thought this man could be a thug. She replied, "He's not going to be a problem. Your rent money took care of that issue."

"As long as your brother paid off the people he owed."

Her jaw dropped.

"It truly wasn't difficult to figure out what had happened, and why he would have rented your property without your permission," Philip said, touching his index finger to her chin and pushing her mouth closed.

Claire swallowed hard, affected by that simple contact far more than she should have been. Shaking off the reaction—Mexican jumping beans in her stomach—she spoke: "He made a mistake. He's young and stupid."

"That much younger than you?"

No, not really. Only five years. But in terms of maturity? She and Freddy had been worlds apart. Claire had had to grow up quickly the first time she'd found their mother passed out from having taken too many pain pills. She'd called 911, then had to go alone to drag her father home from a nearby bar to tell him about it.

She'd been eleven.

"Maybe not in terms of years."

"The real question is, did your brother use the money to pay back his creditors?"

"I'm sure he did."

"Positive?"

"Of course." Oh, she wished her voice held more conviction. Clearing her throat, she added, "Why wouldn't he?"

"Maybe he wanted to use it to go away, escape his problems?"

She gulped. She hadn't heard from Freddy, but assumed it was because he was too much of a chickenshit to face her. Not that he'd… He wouldn't have… Oh, God, would he?

"Sorry." Philip sounded sincere. "You hadn't thought of that."

"No, I hadn't."

"You haven't spoken to him?"

"Not a word."

"Then I'll just continue keeping watch."

"Keeping a… You're watching me?"

"Watching over you," he grudgingly admitted.

"*What?* I'm not some kid who needs protecting."

"Yet protect you I will," he replied, his tone silky, brooking no argument, the words an utter promise. He wasn't asking her, he was telling her. The man was going to look out for her whether she liked it or not.

She was left speechless, simply did not know how to respond to that. Most men she knew barely remembered to hold a door open for a woman, and this one wanted to be her bodyguard because somebody *might* come around looking to collect her brother's debt?

Her independent, free-minded, chicks-rule-and-guys-drool side wanted to tell him to take his protection and his alpha male bullshit and shove them.

But another part of her, maybe the part that went to bed every night thinking of the way this man had held her, kissed her, caught her when she'd nearly fallen on the floor, went all gooey and warm instead.

This would never do. Gooey and warm didn't fit her personality or her life. She was tough and strong. She needed to focus on making her business succeed, on paying her bills, on keeping her brother on the straight-and-narrow.

Claire was the caretaker; she always had been. She wasn't a weeping heroine, a fair maiden who had heroes wanting to look after her. She had no time for overprotective men or fantasies of Prince Charming.

But oh, did he make it tempting.

She cleared her throat and slapped a hand down on the glass countertop. "Is there something you want?"

Me, for instance?

His dark eyes glittered to near black, his mind probably going right where hers had the moment she'd said the words. She kicked herself for giving him that kind of opening.

At least you didn't ask him if he liked your chocolate.

"Yes. There is," he told her.

She stepped back, pulled open the back door of the display case and bent toward it, waiting for him to point something out.

He didn't. He just stood there, looking down at her.

"Do you want to sample something before you decide? I can offer you a free taste."

Seriously? Again? Just tear open your sweater and offer a nipple. That would be about as subtle.

Claire had no idea why the man turned her into an idiot, but had to assume it was because she just hadn't figured him out yet. Or because he kissed like he'd freaking invented kissing.

His lips twitched, as if he'd read her mind and knew she was mad at herself for offering these so-not-subtle innuendos.

"As much as I'd love to *taste* anything you might offer, I actually came here for another reason."

Feeling heat burning her cheeks, she straightened and slid the case closed with a snap. "Oh?"

He nodded. "We've finished moving in, and I find I need to look around the city, to make sure I do want to attend the university here."

"Which one?"

He hesitated. "The New York one."

"New York University—NYU—is a great school." The guy seemed too old for an undergrad, so she assumed he was going for a postgraduate degree. "How can I help?"

"Come out with me and teach me all there is to know about your city."

Her heart thudded. He wasn't here asking for directions, or to buy something to satisfy a sweet tooth. "You want me to…"

"Yes, Claire. I want you to go out with me. Tonight. Now."

She blinked, wondering if that was an invitation, a request or a command. It sounded like all three.

Surprisingly, she hadn't immediately said no. In fact, a hearty *yes* had tried to leap to her lips, but she'd swallowed the word, knowing she shouldn't get any more involved with this man.

"I've got to close the shop."

"It's past closing time," he pointed out.

So it was. She hadn't even noticed. Nor, it appeared, had Jeannie, who was busy chatting up Philip's buddy, who sat at a small café table, his hands curled around a cup of hot coffee.

"I have work to do in the kitchen, orders for tomorrow."

"How long will that take?"

She thought about it. Mrs. West had been working this afternoon and had taken care of the basics. But there were some specialty jobs she didn't trust to anybody but herself. "Probably a couple of hours."

"Very well. Shall we say half past eight?"

A little over two hours from now. Yes, she supposed that was possible. She also supposed it was possible she could get up extra early tomorrow and do the orders. Which would leave her time now to shower, shave her legs, fix her hair, do her makeup, find something fabulous to wear, and talk herself into actually going through with it.

Oh, hell, who was she kidding? Her inner voice—the part of her that didn't always want to be careful and responsible and protective—had already decided.

For once, she wasn't going to be the sensible, always-thinking-of-everyone-else Claire. She was going to think of herself, to do something she *wanted* to do for a change, rather than what she was supposed to do.

She was going to go out with Mr. Dark and Dangerous.

4

"ARE YOU SURE SHE's the one?" asked Shelby a short time later, while Philip got ready. "She's so tall, and unfeminine."

Philip pierced his cousin with a hot glare. "Her strength is part of what makes her so lovely, and she's incredibly feminine in every way that really matters."

He'd known plenty of ultrafeminine—read: helpless—females. Princesses, duchesses, rich merchants' daughters…in his world, they were very much the same. All waited for a man to take care of them. None would risk breaking a nail to fix her own meal, much less spend hours on her feet preparing sweet and pretty treats that customers oohed and aahed over as they left the shop.

Claire's independence fascinated him. Her beauty attracted him. Her wit amused him, her work ethic impressed him and her intelligence challenged him. She filled his thoughts, day and night. Oh, yes. He was sure she was the one.

"All right, then," his cousin said with an exaggerated sigh, throwing himself down on the sagging couch. "It's *your* funeral." Shelby and Teeny made for interesting roommates— he could sometimes hear them bickering through the walls.

Philip just smiled to himself.

At eight-thirty, he walked downstairs to Claire's apartment. The hallway was much brighter than it had been. He'd had Teeny purchase lightbulbs, and had personally installed them, not liking her having to move through the shadows.

Philip knocked once, waited, and knocked again. Then he heard a voice calling along the hall.

"Sorry, I'm here. I wanted to finish up a few things."

Claire was waving to him from the doorway to the sweet shop. He walked toward her, noting the changes in her appearance from when he'd left her a few hours ago.

Though her hair was held back by a clip at one side, she'd left it down, and his hands reflexively tightened at his sides. In the low lighting the other night, he hadn't noticed the hints of copper in the sea of brown curls. The rich swirl of colors brought to mind the decadent caramel chocolates she sold in her shop, and he immediately decided that was his favorite color.

Then she smiled at him, her eyes twinkling, and he remembered blue-green was his favorite color.

Then he looked down and saw the sweater she wore—soft and crimson. Red. *That* was his favorite color.

"I'm ready," she told him. "Just let me lock up."

He waited while she turned to do so, unable to keep his attention from drifting down to the black pants she wore. They were some kind of velvety material—corduroy, he thought it was called—and clung to her curves as if they'd been painted on.

Oh, right. Black is my favorite color.

Hell, he might as well admit it. *She* was his favorite color.

His breath hissed between his teeth as he studied her pert backside, her womanly hips and the length of those incredible legs, which he could almost feel wrapped around his hips.

"Is everything all right?" she asked.

He jerked his attention back to her face, realizing she'd caught him staring. Philip didn't apologize—not because he wasn't used to apologizing for anything, although he was seldom required to. But because he wasn't at all sorry for looking.

She'd worn the clothes so he would look. She'd left her hair down for the same reason. She'd put shadow on her eyelids and shiny gloss on her lips and perfume on her wrists and throat, all to appeal to him. The mating rituals here were no different than in Elatyria. He knew when a woman was trying to appear attractive to a man. Philip didn't tell her that she could still be wearing her apron, with chocolate smeared on her cheek and her hair in a ponytail, and he'd be every bit as attracted.

"Before we go," he said, "there's something I have to do."

Unable to resist, he reached out and slid his hands into her hair, fingering those soft curls. He pulled her to him slowly, giving her every chance to stop him if she desired.

She didn't stop him. So he covered her mouth with his, licking her lips, demanding she open for him. She did, with a sigh, and he swallowed the sound as his tongue thrust gently against hers. Heat rose, excitement flared, and a part of him wanted to suggest the only exploring they do that night was of her bed. But this whole exercise wasn't about bedding a woman. It was about finding his mate—and convincing her that he was right for her, as well. So he regretfully ended the kiss.

He hadn't intended to start the evening that way, but damned if he could say he regretted it. "I've been wanting to do that again since the night we met."

"Truly?"

"Oh, yes."

She hesitated, then spoke softly. "So why haven't you?"

Damn. He knew she'd been wondering about that. He put his hands on her shoulders and looked into her beautiful face, answering honestly. "I had a few obligations to clear up, Claire, and couldn't give you my full attention."

"And now?"

"Now, you've got it. For as long as you want it."

Maybe a lifetime, if his instincts were right. He'd thought she was the one from the moment they met. Every interaction since had convinced him more. Tonight might just confirm it.

She licked her lips, stalling, considering. He didn't think she would respond with a coy rejoinder that perhaps she didn't want it, or tease him that he'd waited too long. She'd never struck him as the kind of woman who played games.

"I'm glad."

He was relieved, and pleased he knew her so well. "Shall we go?"

They left the building and walked in silence for a while, heading toward the bright lights of Times Square.

"What is it you'd like to see?" she eventually asked.

"Everything," he admitted. "Show me what you love about your city. Explain to me why it's beautiful despite being so dirty, why my heart pounds when I smell the strange scents, and why I smile when I see the crush of humanity gathered beneath all these impossibly tall buildings."

She laughed. "You probably appreciate New York more than I do. I've lived here all my life, so it's old hat." Looking up at the lights dominating the skyline, she admitted, "I like seeing it fresh, through your eyes."

So they showed the city to each other. For the next two hours, they explored the "Big Apple," though he didn't know why she called it that. They walked up Broadway and saw the theater marquees competing for space with the kitschy tourist shops. They were encouraged to try free samples, to come in and check out prices, to accept coupons for "no cover" in clubs from pushy barkers.

One of them got too aggressive with Claire, blocking her

path and then putting a hand on her arm. Seeing red, Philip reacted instinctively. He shoved his way between them, taking the man's wrist in one hand and his shoulder in the other, and propelled him out onto the street.

After that, Philip kept his hand on the small of her back as they maneuvered through the crowd, ever so aware of the warmth of her body beneath her coat. He was also aware of every laugh, every smile, of the way her eyes gleamed as she gazed up at the big, brightly decorated tree in front of Rockefeller Center.

They talked about nothing of importance, but he couldn't remember ever laughing more. Claire was caustic and a little outrageous, but also smart, warm and charming.

He found himself telling her about his own background— as much as he could without revealing he was a prince from another dimension. Somehow, though, families were the same in every world, and in every income bracket, and he soon had her laughing when he described the way his mother ruled the house—and kingdom—while letting his father think he did.

There was only one thing on which they disagreed. Fascinated by a store called Hershey's, which was, apparently, filled with nothing but chocolate, Philip reluctantly let Claire tug him away.

"I've got plenty of candy at home for you to try," she said.

Damn. Did she do that on purpose? Did she know that when she said "candy," he was thinking about her sweet lips and creamy skin?

A flush appeared in her cheeks. Yes. She knew.

"Sorry," she mumbled.

"You can't apologize for being delicious."

She stopped midstride, and someone walking behind her almost crashed into her.

"Hey, watch it, dumb-ass!"

Philip swung around, fire in his eyes. The young man

who'd spoken flinched, mumbled an apology and moved around them.

But their easy laughter and casual conversation faded away. The awareness that had existed from that first moment in the back of her candy shop returned full force, a tangible thing between them. Claire was quiet, wouldn't meet his eye, and he sighed deeply.

Finally, she confirmed she'd had enough. "We should probably get back," she told him. "It's getting late."

"Very well."

They walked in silence again. Eventually, Philip cleared his throat. "I apologize for making you feel uncomfortable."

Instead of acknowledging that, she actually giggled. "So you *are* capable of apologizing! I figured you just always offered, but never actually did it."

He joined in her laughter because, yes, that had happened a few times since they'd met.

By the time they reached their building, they'd fallen back into casual conversation. Light, friendly, absolutely nothing about candy or deliciousness or how very much he wanted to touch her. Philip knew he'd pushed too hard, and she'd stepped back. He didn't want to make that mistake again.

Walking her to her door, he fully expected her to say goodnight. But to his surprise, she said something else instead.

"I believe I owe you some chocolate…since I wouldn't let you go in and buy any from that other store."

She'd obviously added that last part to make sure he didn't mistake her words for any kind of innuendo. "Yes, you do."

"Do you like brownies?"

"I'm not sure."

She gasped. "You've never had brownies?"

"I don't think so," he admitted.

"Oh, buddy, have I got a treat for you. Come on, I made a batch earlier…and I happen to have vanilla ice cream. A little melted Godiva and we are *so* on for hot fudge brownie sundaes!"

"Godiva… Is that what you were melting the night we met?"

"Uh-huh."

He grinned. "We are *so* on for hot fudge brownie sundaes."

SHE SHOULD HAVE SAID good-night.

The smart thing to do—the sane thing, considering she had no time for a relationship with anyone, much less a guy who made her forget she had a brain cell in her head—would have been to shake Philip's hand and walk away.

Instead, Claire found herself in the kitchen making sundaes with a man.

"I think I've died and gone to heaven," he said as he leaned over to sniff the pot on the big, industrial stove, in which she was whipping up a special hot fudge topping. "I could swim in a pool of that and never come out."

Mmm. A pool of dark, decadent chocolate and this dark, decadent man. Sounded like a delicious combination to her.

"Almost ready." She continued to stir the hot fudge. "Will you please grab the ice cream from the walk-in freezer?"

He glanced around, one eyebrow lifted as if he didn't know what a walk-in freezer looked like. She had never realized how different Spain must be from the United States. She nodded toward the freezer, and he went in, returning a moment later with the large, unopened container.

"Let's let it soften up a little, okay? By the time it's soft enough to scoop, the fudge sauce will have cooled off just a bit and we'll be able to eat it."

"You're very knowledgeable about this," he said.

"It's my job," she answered with a shrug.

"How did you get started in this career?"

"I've always loved baking and candy-making. My grandmother was a fantastic cook and I used to work with her in the kitchen all the time. She started me on her famous chocolate-dipped peanut brittle when I was eight, and I never looked back."

Claire walked over to the counter and settled on a stool. He sat opposite her, dropping his elbows onto the surface and clasping his hands together. Such big hands, strong and powerful. She still couldn't get over how easily he'd handled that obnoxious barker, how he'd lifted the burly man off his toes as he'd thrust him out of the way. Philip might not be the brawny enforcer she'd first imagined him to be, but he was strong.

"Did your grandmother help you start this shop?"

"She passed away years ago. Before my parents did."

"Both of them?"

"Yes. It's just me and Freddy now."

Philip's expression hardened. "I take it your brother's not much help."

"He'll grow up one of these days."

"So, you did all this by yourself?" Philip asked, looking around the immaculate, state-of-the-art kitchen.

"With the help of some contractors and workmen, yes, I did."

"Impressive." Admiration shone on his face.

"What do you think of my city now?" she inquired, changing the subject.

"Also impressive."

"What's *most* impressive? The crowds, the pickpockets, the rotten garbage, the honking taxis, the screaming drivers or the clueless tourists?" All of which they'd seen during their two-hour track through the touristy Broadway district. All of which she'd enjoyed, as crazy as it was. It was home to her, but usually turned other people off.

Philip hadn't seemed the least bit bothered by any of it.

"Are those attributes?" he asked, a twinkle in his eye.

"Definitely."

"Then no wonder this city has captivated me," he said, sounding as if he meant it. "I love the seediness of it."

"If you like seediness, you must get to New Orleans."

"Very well. When should we go?"

Grinning, she played along. "Three Christmases from now?"

"It's a date."

"Do you really think you'll be around then?" she murmured, pretending she wasn't terribly interested in his answer.

"That depends."

"On what?"

"On how things unfold once I get back home. If all goes as I hope, I should be coming back to America to visit quite often."

She'd like that. A lot.

Realizing the ice cream was probably soft enough to scoop, she went over to the other counter. Philip watched her as she cut two healthy pieces from the pan of brownies, put them into bowls, then plopped heaping spoonfuls of ice cream on top. When she headed over to get the chocolate sauce, however, he joined her.

"This I want to do," he murmured.

"You really are a chocolate fiend."

"Proudly."

"Most guys think chocolate addiction is a chick thing."

"Do you think I'm like most guys?"

Watching him drizzle chocolate over the ice cream, his hand strong and steady, muscles flexing in his forearm, she shook her head. "No. I don't think you're like anyone I've ever met."

Realizing she'd grown too serious, she helped herself to half as much hot fudge as he'd taken, then carried her bowl back to the counter. Philip joined her, and for the next few minutes said nothing. He savored every drop of warm choc-olate, creamy ice cream and soft brownie. She'd swear the man's expression was orgasmic, and he moaned pleasurably as he ate.

Claire had never imagined it would be a complete turn-on to watch a man eat dessert. But the way he so carefully and thoroughly tasted everything, closing his eyes and letting the cool cream glide down his throat, or licking the last bit of chocolate off his spoon, soon had her shifting on her seat. Her pulse was throbbing in her veins, and it had nothing to do with sugar, everything to do with spice.

Philip Smith was just so damned hot and exotic, so dif-ferent from any man she'd known before. He held nothing back—not his appreciation for her, not his enjoyment of his food, not his delight in the crowds and the noise and the frenzy of the city. He was…sensual. That was it. The man was entirely in tune with his senses, and she found that in-credibly sexy.

Claire wasn't quite sure what was happening to her. Sure, she'd had relationships before, mostly brief, but one long-term one that had lasted through two years of college. But she'd never felt so totally in tune with another person's sensual re-sponses as she did right now, with him.

"You have chocolate on your mouth," he said.

"Do I?" She licked her lips.

"No," he told her, leaning across the counter until his face was inches from hers. "It's here."

He didn't wipe it off with his hand or a napkin. Instead, he moved his mouth to the corner of hers and kissed her, his tongue flicking out to sample the smudge she'd left behind.

"Mmm," he murmured as their lips brushed. "You taste good."

She knew it wasn't smart, knew it was too soon and that she'd only recently met him. But common sense seemed to have departed for the night. So without a word, she reached up and put her arms around his neck, parting her lips and inviting him to deepen his kiss.

He did, his cold, sweet tongue tangling with hers in slow, hungry thrusts. He tasted so delicious, made the chocolate more rich, the ice cream more sweet, the brownie more decadent. Claire tilted her head, wanting their mouths locked more tightly together, and the kiss deepened, grew hotter, wetter.

Before she realized what was happening, Philip had gotten up, reached over and pulled her to her feet. He dropped his hands to her waist and lifted her onto the counter before him, her legs dangling over the edge.

Claire didn't resist; she was putty in his hands. He moved her easily, as if she weighed nothing, and his strength boggled her mind.

He pulled her close to his big, hard body, until she was sitting directly in front of him. Dropping his hands onto her parted thighs, he stepped between them and proceeded to kiss her again.

The hunger erupted. She felt his heat, his breadth, his strength, pressed against her, and desperately wanted to feel all those things without the barrier of clothing. The kiss was devouring, demanding. He lifted both hands and sank them into her hair, cupping her head, keeping her where he wanted her.

It was a long kiss. "You taste better than the chocolate," he said when it ended. His voice was thick with desire.

Feeling drugged, intoxicated, she replied, "So do you."

Without saying another word, Philip reached for his bowl and swiped his finger through the melted chocolate and ice cream. He traced his fingertip down the side of her neck, from just below her ear to the hollow of her throat.

"Ooh, cold," she said, knowing she wouldn't be for long.

"I'll warm you," he promised as he bent down and kissed

her neck. And he did, sparking a flame as he licked away the chocolate and the creaminess, sampling her skin, tasting her all the way down. He devoured her with the same care and deliberation he'd used on his dessert, and all she could think was how very much she wanted him to do it again.

"Hmm, my bowl's wiped clean," he muttered, sounding disappointed. He cast a look across the kitchen at the stove. The pot of hot fudge was still there, off the heat, probably cool and congealing by now. Perfect for playing with. "Don't move."

Claire held her breath, watching as he jogged over to get the pot, tested it with his fingertip, then carried it back. His steps slowed as he returned, his gaze fixed on her face, his eyes darkening with passion.

She knew where this was going. Knew what he wanted. Knew what he intended to do. And she wanted it, too. All of it.

He stopped a few feet away, lifting a brow in question.

She reached up and brushed the tips of her fingers over the hollow of her throat, then trailed them downward to the deep V-neck of her sweater.

That was all the assent he required. Philip's smile was sultry, his movements deliberate and seductive as he moved in front of her. He put the pot down beside her, then swirled his finger in the thickening mass of slick, dark sweetness.

This time, the line of chocolate he drew went from her throat all the way down to the curves of her breasts, traveling the same path her fingers had.

"Oh." She sighed, incredibly aroused by just that touch, knowing his hands would soon be replaced by his mouth.

He moved to her throat, growling as he licked the chocolate from her skin, working his way down…down…until his face was pressed into her cleavage. She was trembling now, her hands clenching his shoulders as she anticipated so much more.

She didn't even pretend to resist when he reached for the bottom hem of her sweater and drew it up and off. Sitting there in only her pants and a lacy, sexy red bra she'd donned just in case she might have reason to take her sweater off tonight, she watched him study her. Watched his dark eyes grow nearly black and his mouth open to release an unsteady breath.

Desire seemed to drip from the man, a physical, tangible thing. And all directed at her.

"I like this." He ran a knuckle over her bra strap.

"You'll like it even more when it's where it belongs."

"Where does it belong?"

"On the floor."

He licked his lips, reached for the front clasp of her bra and flicked it with his thumb and forefinger. The fabric fell apart, her full, aching breasts nearly revealed to his covetous stare. She saw the way his jaw clenched, and knew he very much liked what he saw. But instead of pulling the bra the rest of the way off, he reached for the hot fudge again.

Trembles turned to quivers. This time, he used two fingers to scoop up a heaping helping of the chocolate. Claire held her breath, not sure where he'd move them, wondering if he intended to ice her body like a cake and devour her completely.

She'd be okay with that. This man could call her his own personal devil's food for as long as he liked.

He finally returned his hand to the moist spot between her breasts where he'd last had his mouth. He slowly drew a swirling infinity sign, his talented fingers edging the bra out of the way as he painted a trail of warm chocolate over each breast, around each areola, leaving just the puckered tips uncovered.

"Those are sweet enough. They don't need any topping," he murmured, gazing at her distended nipples.

She shifted on the countertop, her sex throbbing and wet. She was so hot for him it was painful to sit on the hard surface.

He began to lick away the trail he'd created. Claire curled her fingers in his hair, needing to keep herself steady as he sampled her skin. The brush of his sandpapery cheek against the side of her breast made her groan. When his lips came close to an uncovered nipple, she wanted to beg. But he moved past, following the chocolate, leaving her nipples pouty, full, untasted.

"Oh, God, please," she whimpered.

He didn't relent, licking every inch of chocolate off her breasts before making the slightest move toward the most sensitive tips. She was ready to weep by the time he finally gazed hungrily at one pouty nipple. And she cried out when, without warning, he planted his mouth there, covered it and sucked deeply.

"Yes!" she groaned.

As if knowing how aroused she was, and how badly she needed his attention, he lifted his hand to her other breast. He squeezed lightly, stroking the nipple between his strong fingers, then tweaked it, toyed with it, all while suckling her. Waves of heat plummeted through her core and she had to wriggle on the countertop. The seam of her tight cords was pressed against her clit, which was swollen, a bundle of nerves.

"Lie back," he ordered, his lips still against her breast.

She sucked in a breath, unsure for a moment. This man wanted her to lay herself out like a feast? He desired her that much?

"Please, Claire."

"I do have a bedroom."

"That'll take too long. Let me adore you, here and now."

Adore her? The man's voice was velvety and assured, his expression hungry and passionate. He wanted her to *let* him adore her, when, by rights, she should be on her knees begging him not to stop.

As if stopping was in the realm of possibility.

Maybe for the sensible Claire, the one who always took care of everyone else, it would be. But that part of her had disappeared tonight. She had never imagined she would like strong, overprotective men. But somewhere between Philip insisting that he take her out, admitting he'd been watching her, tossing that obnoxious barker out of her path and urging her to *let* him, Claire had realized she wanted nothing more than to give over control to someone else for a change. Maybe not for long—perhaps just for tonight—but she was ready to let go, to be taken care of.

To be adored.

5

MELTING LIKE THE chocolate, all reservations gone, Claire shimmied to the middle of the countertop, kicking her shoes to the floor. As instructed, she lowered herself on her back, moving slowly. Philip helped her, stroking her tenderly, kissing his way down her middle.

"Trust me," he urged, as if thinking she might still have reservations about putting herself so completely at his mercy.

"I do," she admitted. She hadn't met him very long ago, but already knew him a strong, sexy, honorable, funny, intelligent man. He wouldn't hurt her. Of that she had no doubt.

Once she was comfortable, he scooped up more chocolate and drew a line straight down her midriff, letting a few drops fall into her belly button. Then he licked it all away, kissing her, nibbling her sensitive skin, tenderly exploring her navel.

She didn't demur when he reached for the waistband of her pants, unbuttoned and unzipped them, and began to draw them down. She lifted her hips, helping free the material, watching the hunger on his face turn to raw lust. He stared avariciously at the hollow just above her pubic bone, at the lacy edge of her red panties. A hungry sigh emerged from his mouth when he uncovered her hips and filled his hands with them, squeezing lightly. Then he continued to pull her pants down, stroking her thighs and calves as he pulled them off.

He stopped and stared at her, lying there in nothing but a skimpy pair of underwear, through which he had to be able to see the tuft of dark curls. He rubbed his hand against his jaw.

"I've fantasized about seeing you unclothed."

"Right back at you," she admitted.

"That might have to wait. I'm not *prepared* for this."

Hell. She hadn't thought of birth control. Claire wasn't even sure she had any condoms in her apartment. It had been months since she'd had sex. She hadn't even been living in the building then.

Philip must have seen her disappointment. "I'll never be caught without what I need again, but for right now, I'll just have to make it up to you in other ways."

Oh, goodness. That was a pure, sultry promise in his voice.

"We can make it up to each other," she purred, reaching for him.

He grabbed her wrists, stopping her. "Me first."

Lordy, the man was hot when he was being bossy.

"There is much I want to do."

Right. He had a lot of things to do. Delicious, delightful, sinful, wicked things.

He proceeded to do them. Claire lost all inhibition, didn't think about the fact that she was spread out like a virgin sacrifice at a banquet of the gods. She was a slave to sensation, unsure where he would smear the next dollop of warm chocolate, holding her breath in anticipation until he licked it clean away.

By the time he got to her groin and breathed hotly through the lacy panties, she was thrusting her hips up, unable to control the demands of her body. He put a hand on her hip, holding her in place while he smoothed more chocolate right over the lace. As he licked it off, the rasp and warmth of his tongue sent her flying out of control. Pulses of pleasure washed through her and she felt her climax build.

"Wait." His tone demanded obedience. "I'm not finished."

"Are you kidding me?" she wailed.

"Do not let it happen," he insisted, looking up at her, his dark eyes intense. "Hold back—you won't regret it."

She had never intentionally tried to stop herself from coming, especially since not every lover she'd been with had even been able to bring her to orgasm. But the look in Philip's eyes swore he wouldn't let her down, and promised it would be worth the wait.

She closed her eyes and took a few deep, steadying breaths, trying to slow her racing heart, counting each pulse in her throbbing clit. She whimpered when he slid his fingers under the elastic of her panties and slowly drew them down. They hadn't provided much covering, but once they were gone and she was completely naked, bared before a fully dressed man in a cool room, she shivered.

"No, you're not cold. You're burning up."

He was right. The air might be cool, but she was absolutely on fire, the temperature going up by degrees every second he stared at her with that wanton, hungry look.

He reached for the chocolate. "This can't taste as good as you do, but it would be a shame to let it go to waste."

She held her breath. He scooped some up and moved his hand between her thighs. Slick, slippery warmth smoothed over the lips of her sex, and she cooed. "Oh, Philip!"

"Hold on. Wait for it...."

"I'm trying," she said, wondering how much pleasure a human body could stand. Because this was utterly divine.

His fingers delved deeper, spreading her, stroking her. She chewed her bottom lip, shocked at how good it felt—his strong fingers wrapped in silky warmth, caressing her clit in delicate circles. Taking her higher and higher, but never over the top. And she suddenly realized the pressure she usually felt to hurry up and come had receded. The climax was worth waiting for because this buildup was so incredibly good. He was coaxing her up step by step, rather than pushing her, in a mad race to get to the top.

Finally, he slipped one finger into her, sliding deep, her own body's juices and the chocolate making his penetration easy.

"Philip, yes," she cried.

Another finger joined in, stretching her, filling her slowly, then gliding away. She loved the fullness and the heat, the way he found a sensitive spot high inside her and brought it to life. Loved the look on his face and the sound of his whispers and the feel of his warm breath as he bent closer to her sex.

"I want to taste you as you come."

"Please…"

"Shh," he told her, moving his lips ever nearer. He didn't go right to her clit, but started lower, tasting all that chocolate, pulling his fingers away so he could slide his tongue inside her and lap up every bit.

This time there would be no stopping the climax. Claire couldn't prevent a tiny wail of helpless delight as it barreled toward her. Hearing her, Philip moved up, finally sliding his tongue over her clit in a thorough exploration that set her rocketing to the pinnacle.

She thrust up to meet him, her orgasm setting her free. It was powerful, making her shake, and he moved his fingers back into her tight channel, which spasmed around him while he savored the chocolate and her body's juices like a man at a feast.

One orgasm stretched into two. She'd no sooner begun to settle back to earth when he sucked again, a little harder, and another ratcheted out of nowhere.

"Oh, my God," she cried.

She'd never experienced anything like it, never been hit with pleasure after pleasure. He'd been right; holding off, letting her own desires build to the utter peak, made flying off that peak better than it had ever been in her life.

She'd barely begun to breathe normally when Philip kissed his way back up her body, then leaned right over her face. She smelled chocolate and sex on his breath. Wanting to share, she reached up and twined her fingers in his hair, pulling his mouth to hers. They exchanged a long, wicked kiss.

"I've never experienced anything like that," she whispered when they finally drew apart. "Nobody's ever made me feel…"

"Then the men you've known are fools," he declared.

He was no fool, though. He was bloody close to perfection. "You…you didn't mind…"

He barked a laugh. "Are you joking? You taste so good, Claire. So sweet and perfect. I've never eaten anything so delicious in my entire life. I could dine on you and nothing else until the day I die, and never be hungry again."

That sounded all well and good. But she was hungry, too.

He might not be able to make love to her tonight, but damned if she was going to let him leave without her seeing the magnificent body beneath his clothes.

"My turn," she insisted as she sat up. She wrapped her legs around him before he could back away.

"Claire…"

She pressed a hot, openmouthed kiss to his lips. "I know how far we can go," she whispered.

And she proceeded to go there. She reached for his long-sleeved shirt and pulled it up, her breath catching in her throat as she beheld the miles of gleaming skin covering a pair of massive shoulders and a powerful chest. He was roped with muscle, beautifully formed. She stroked him with her fingertips, a little amazed, a little stunned. As if driven, she reached out and tangled her fingers in the sparse, wiry black hair on his chest, scratching her nails over his flat nipples, drawing a hiss.

"You are perfect," she whispered as she ran her hands down, to toy with the trail of hair that led to the waistband of his jeans.

When she reached for his belt buckle, he put his hand over hers. "You don't have to—"

"Yes, I do." She stared intently into his eyes, seeing the passion, the need he couldn't disguise. "I'm desperate to."

His breaths quickened, but he didn't try to stop her as she unfastened his jeans. Unable to reach him, or see nearly as much as she wanted to, she got down from the counter to stand before him, letting her naked breasts brush against his broad chest. Her nipples were still sensitive from arousal, from his heated caresses, and she sighed at the rightness of it, hearing his groan of appreciation.

Claire bit her lip as she unzipped his pants, her hand starting to shake as she felt the huge, powerful erection under his fly. Her breath caught when she saw the tip of his cock peeking above the waistband of his boxer briefs.

"Oh, God," she groaned, shocked at how big, hard and gorgeous he was. She slid her palm over the head, spreading the moisture there, and then reached inside his briefs to wrap as much of her hand around him as she could.

"Ah, Claire, you feel wonderful."

"You are amazing," she told him, loving the way he dropped his head back as she stroked him, up, then down, loving the thickness of him in her hand. She was also unhappy that she couldn't have that thickness in her pulsing, throbbing vagina. But she wasn't about to send him back upstairs unsatisfied.

"I'm still hungry," she said, reaching for the chocolate sauce.

"You owe me nothing."

"This isn't about owing," she informed him as she slowly lowered herself to her knees, setting the pot on the floor beside her. "It's simply about wanting to taste your cock."

He thrust his hands in her hair, his hips jerking reflexively as if her words had utterly inflamed him. Well, good. That had been the point. Plus they'd been true.

She tugged his pants and boxer briefs down, then had to just kneel in front of him for a moment, staring at the massive, proud erection rising from a dark thatch beneath. She scraped her fingernails along his powerful thighs, trying to remember to breathe, wondering if she'd ever be able to take him into her body, much less in her mouth.

She was certainly going to give it her best shot.

She leaned over and flicked her tongue against the base of his shaft, hearing his groan of pleasure. Then she did it again, this time swirling the tip over his vulnerable sac before sliding it up the length of him.

His hands twisted and tangled in her hair, though he didn't pull her or hurt her in any way. He seemed to like how it felt, because he lifted a few long strands and rubbed them on his bare stomach.

Claire barely noticed, focused only on kissing her way up the length of him. When she finally got to the top, she flicked her tongue out to taste the fluid leaking from him, drawing another groan from his chest.

The chocolate could wait. For now, she just wanted to taste man. She opened her mouth as far as she could and sucked him in.

"Gods, Claire, that feels amazing."

She didn't respond, focused only on laving the engorged head. She sucked him hard while she wrapped her hand around the breadth of him and stroked, up and down. She took him as deep as she could, working him with her hands, building his frenzy.

Eventually, wanting to experience what he had, by mixing decadent food with decadent pleasure, she reached for the chocolate sauce and scooped up a handful. She looked up at him, watching him watch her, his dark eyes gleaming, his face racked with emotion and hunger. He said nothing as she curled her chocolate-smeared hand around him and stroked some more. Then she moved her mouth back to the tip of him to swallow up that sweetness and masculine heat.

"You'll unman me."

"That's the plan," she mumbled as she stroked and sucked.

His whole body seemed to grow harder, his muscles flexing, straining, a sheen of sweat highlighting every perfect ridge and slope. He was panting now, striving toward his climax, and she kept pace, stroking harder, sucking deeper.

"Claire!" he cried out, and tried to push her back.

She wasn't having that. The chocolate and the sweat and the cum and the heat were utterly intoxicating. She was greedy for all of it. So she held tight, her fingers digging into his hips as she forced him to plunge harder into her mouth, driving toward her throat. Until at last a guttural cry signaled his orgasm.

He came in a hot gush and she swallowed greedily, shocked and fascinated at how much she enjoyed this, when she never had before. Something about this big, strong man being made vulnerable because of her, receiving his ultimate pleasure and spewing all that power into her mouth, made her feel strong, confident and surprisingly feminine.

They'd offered each other pleasure, but they'd also given and exchanged sexual power. It was like nothing she'd ever experienced. And as Philip drew her to her feet, wrapped his arms around her waist and pulled her to him for a deep, tender kiss, she began to suspect that it wasn't the act itself that had been so erotic and blissful…it had been that act with this perfect, incredible man.

IT WAS VERY LATE by the time Philip returned to his apartment. After that intense oral pleasure, he and Claire had thoroughly scrubbed the kitchen, then gone back to her apartment down the hall. He'd been incredibly tempted by her offer of a hot, steamy shower together, but once she'd searched her place and realized she had no sexual protection, he'd kissed her good-night and taken his leave. If they'd gotten naked again, he wouldn't have been able to stop himself from possessing her. And he suspected she wouldn't have wanted him to.

A trip to the nearest store was first thing on his list for morning.

"Well, how was it?" a voice asked as he reached his door.

He glanced over his shoulder and saw both his compatriots, peeking at him from across the hall. Teeny was so much taller, his gleaming round eyes were a good foot above Shelby's.

"We had a…very nice evening," Philip said, hearing the satisfaction in his own voice. He didn't elaborate. What he and Claire had shared was nobody else's business but their own.

"Is it settled, then? Is she the one?" asked Shelby.

Philip didn't even have to think about it. "She is most definitely the one." Whatever feelings he'd had for Claire before paled in comparison to what he felt for her now. Having spent so many hours in her company—some just walking and talking, some being more intimate than any he'd ever spent in his life—he knew he was falling in love with her.

"When is the wedding?" Teeny asked, his expression as close to happy as it ever got.

Philip laughed softly. "I haven't even proposed to her yet."

"Well, why not?" Shelby let out an annoyed sigh. "You know she is the one, so tell her who we are, and we can get out of here."

"I have to court her."

Shelby blew out a rude sound. "Just give her some diamonds. That'll convince her."

"Have you forgotten that the entire reason we came here was so I could make sure my future bride loves me for myself, not for what I can bestow upon her?"

His cousin suddenly snapped his fingers. "That reminds me! You will never believe what Teeny and I watched on that television device tonight! It was your story!"

Teeny piped up. "It was quite remarkable, Your Highness, as if some performers had decided to act out your life."

Curious, Philip waited for an explanation.

"It was a film," Shelby explained, nodding his head and sounding knowledgeable—as if he knew all there was to know about this world already. "A film about a prince and his very handsome, talented, witty, well-dressed manservant, coming to America to find the prince a bride who would love him for himself."

Shocked, Philip felt his mouth fall open. "What happens?"

"They go to work in a fast-food restaurant, mopping floors, and live in a tenement building much like this one."

Teeny broke in again. "At one point, the manservant pretends to be the prince and woos the heroine's sister with talk of his—the real prince's—wealth."

Shelby glared up at the bodyguard. "That's beside the point."

"Don't you dare," Philip warned his cousin.

"I wouldn't dream of it!"

Sure he wouldn't.

"Does the prince win the maiden?" Philip asked.

"He does, Your Highness, although he fears all is lost when she finds out he has been lying to her. In fact, he goes back to his kingdom in sadness and disappointment, and it isn't until he is at the altar about to wed another that he realizes she has come after him."

Claire wouldn't be able to come after him if Philip left without her. As of right now, she didn't even know his world existed. Few on Earth did, though most Elatyrians knew about their neighboring world, some even moving back and forth between them on a weekly basis. But she certainly would have no way of finding it.

"Are you saying I need to tell her the truth?" he asked.

Teeny nodded and Shelby did too the very same instant. These two never agreed on anything.

Philip answered his own question. "I will," he stated firmly. "I need just a few more days, then I'll be completely honest with her and ask her to come back with me to Elatyria."

"She'll say yes," Shelby insisted loyally.

Teeny didn't look so sure.

"What is it?" Philip asked the frowning man.

"Well, that brother of hers…"

"Have you seen him?"

"I saw him," Teeny admitted. "He and another man were up the block this afternoon. Mr. Freddy was pointing toward the shop, appearing nervous and guilty."

Philip's blood raced through his veins. He could think of no reason for Claire's brother to be skulking around, showing people where she lived and worked, unless he was in more trouble and was counting on his sister to get him out of it.

It was time to teach that pup a lesson. Past time.

But until Philip got hold of him, it was back to full-time guard duty for him and his friends.

"I know, I know," Shelby said, as if reading his mind. "I'll take the first watch tonight. Teeny will relieve me in four hours. I assume you intend to guard her tomorrow?"

"I certainly do," Philip said. He'd planned to give her some time, to perhaps wait until late afternoon to stop in and see how she was feeling about things, after all that had happened tonight. Now, knowing she might be in danger, he couldn't afford to wait. "Thank you, my friends."

Murmuring good night, Philip went into his sorry little apartment, which, he had to admit, looked much better than it had ten days ago, when he'd first seen it. Though he hadn't spent a great deal of money, in case Claire or anyone else should come up and wonder how he could afford it, he and his friends had invested some physical labor. It had felt good to scour, fix walls, seal windows and clean. Philip was used to a lot of physical activity at home—mainly riding, jousting, and occasionally leading a battle against the brigands who sometimes invaded the kingdom from the desert. Other than walking around the city, he'd had no outlet for his pent-up energy here, so working on these rooms had been cathartic.

He wondered what Claire would think when she saw them. He also wondered how she'd feel about leaving this behind.

Part of him suspected she would not want to go, since she appeared devoted to her small shop. But there were candy shops in his world, too, and while she might be the first royal princess to have a job, that's what she would have if that's what she wanted.

First, though, he had to convince her to come with him. Which wouldn't be a problem if she truly fell in love with him.

The question was, would she? And did he have enough time for her to?

His month of freedom was more than halfway over. He had to leave a few days at the end for the return, and had already decided he would have to depart New York City on Christmas Eve to make it home in time. Which meant he had less than two weeks to capture the love of the woman who'd win his.

He'd possessed her body tonight—and the memory of what they'd shared would haunt his dreams and his fantasies for the rest of his life. Now he needed to lay siege to her heart.

6

THOUGH SHE WOULD NEVER regret the incredibly sensual interlude she'd shared with Philip, Claire couldn't help wishing it
hadn't been a workday. Because the next morning, she was
weary and dragging. She felt drugged. Maybe she'd OD'd
on chocolate.

"But oh, God, what a way to go," she whispered as she put
the finishing touches on some beautifully decorated sugared
plums. She'd already been at work for two hours, finishing
up the special orders she'd neglected the night before, and
realized it was time to open the shop.

After starting the industrial-size coffeepots, she lifted the
chairs off the small tables and set them in place. Then she
pulled open the blinds and went to unlock the door, flipping
the sign from Closed to Open.

Through the glass, she was surprised to see a small line
of people waiting outside.

"Please come in!"

She stepped back and gestured for them to step in out of the
blustery morning air. Claire had been in business for almost
a month now, but this was the first time people had actually
been waiting for her to open. She couldn't contain a rush of
pleasure and satisfaction at having come this far, this quickly.

With a smile on her face, she served coffee and pastries—something she'd recently added to the menu to appeal to the breakfast crowd. Plus there were plenty of order pickups, orders placed, and on-the-spot treats purchased.

It wasn't until nearly eleven that she had a chance to sit down, feeling both exhausted and energized, somehow. And of course, that was the moment when her lover—well, her oral lover, anyway, since they hadn't taken that oh-so-intimate final step—walked through the door.

As always, Philip filled up the room. He had such presence, an almost regal air. His amazing body was always perfectly straight, his jaw tilted slightly as his beautiful bedroom eyes surveyed the room. The guy could part a crowd—she'd seen that last night—and could dominate a large space. Suddenly, the walls seemed much closer, the room more intimate, and the setting far more private than a shop that had been filled with people ten minutes ago.

"Good morning, Claire," he said, that throaty voice almost purring. "Did you sleep well?"

Thinking of the night's sleep she had—of the erotic dreams he'd inspired and the way she'd been shaken awake from one of them by a powerful orgasm—she felt color flood into her cheeks.

"Oh. I see you did," he said, a small smile playing on that sensuous mouth she had grown to adore.

"Yes. And you?"

"Not really," he admitted.

Her stomach lurched. Had she been the only one affected by the incredible intimacies they'd shared? "No?"

"I could think only about the coming of morning, when the sundry store around the corner would open for business."

Not understanding, she tipped her head in confusion.

Philip lifted his hand to show her the small plastic bag he

was carrying. She peered at it, able to just make out the lettering on the small box within.

"That's… Oh," she whispered, her legs suddenly wobbly as she realized he'd gone out first thing this morning to buy a box of condoms.

"You approve?"

She nodded vehemently. "I most definitely approve."

He appeared relieved. Good grief, had he really been wondering if she'd had second thoughts? If, after having that amazing mouth and those remarkable hands bring her to the height of pleasure, she would possibly not want more? Only an insane woman—or one without a hint of estrogen—could have been pressed up against that hot, sexy male body, could have seen that massive, proud erection, could have tasted the heat of him, and not wanted more.

Philip cast another glance around the shop, as if to make sure no one else was there, and strode toward her. Wrapping his arms around her, he hauled her against him for a deep, hungry good-morning kiss. His body was so big, broad and warm, his kiss so devouring and demanding, she couldn't help but melt against him, kissing him back with every ounce of passion he'd aroused in her the night before. Both during their amazing kitchen interlude and in her dreams.

"I thought about you all night long," he admitted.

"Ditto."

He raised a curious brow.

"I mean, me, too," she explained, liking the way he sometimes didn't understand her way of speaking. He was old-fashioned in some respects, almost otherworldly at times. She liked that about him. Hell, she liked everything about him. Every damn thing, from the way he looked to the way he talked to the sound of his husky laugh, to the light in his eyes, to his brainy conversation, to the way he used his mouth…everywhere.

He intoxicated her. Aroused her. Thrilled her.

She was falling for this man, hard and fast. And somehow, the logical, care-taking Claire, who should have already put on the brakes, since she had little time or room in her life for a relationship, was keeping her big fat mouth shut. The Claire who sometimes dreamed of more, who fantasized about true love and happily-ever-after, was strictly in charge.

"So when's closing time?"

A gurgle of laughter rose in her throat as she heard the boyish anticipation in his tone. She suspected that box of condoms would be burning a hole through the bag, from all the heated thoughts sent its way.

"I usually stay open later on Wednesday evenings, so not until eight."

"Your assistant—is she working today?"

"Uh-huh."

"And the lady who is helping with the cooking?"

"Yes, Mrs. West will be in, too. She's fantastic."

"I'm glad to hear it," he said with a satisfied smile, as if he'd personally selected the woman for the job. "So can you, perhaps, leave a little early?"

"I'm sorry. I've been so busy already, I honestly doubt it."

"Hmm... What if I got someone else to help man the store?"

"Your mastodon in the china shop? I don't think so."

"No, not Teeny. I mean Shelby."

Remembering the slightly snooty guy who'd been flirting with Jeannie the day before, Claire scrunched her brow. "I doubt he'd—"

"Oh, he'd love to," Philip insisted with a nod. "He was just telling me this morning how much he'd love to learn more about business. And about candy. About the candy business."

That didn't sound like the man she'd met. "Seriously?"

"Indeed. He's quite anxious to learn. You would be doing

him a favor by allowing him to be your employee's assistant tonight. And then you could leave early and come with me."

Claire wrapped her arms around Philip's neck and smiled up at him. "Where? All the way back to my bedroom?"

"No," he said, dropping his hands to her hips and stroking gently. "I have arranged a surprise for us."

Ooh, that sounded interesting. And very tempting.

"Well, if it's just for an hour or so, I suppose I could—"

"Excellent. It's settled. I will meet you here at six o'clock." He kissed her forehead. "Dress up."

There was that bossy tone again.

"Are you sure you can afford for us to go somewhere that requires 'dressing up'?" In New York, dinner at a fancy restaurant could cost a lot of money, and on his visiting student income, she didn't want him to overextend himself.

"I wasn't entirely forthcoming with you about my finances," he admitted. "I'm perhaps not quite as poor as I let on."

She'd suspected as much, given the way he dressed and his confident manner. "So why did you say you were?"

"Because I wanted to stay here, in this building." He dropped his mouth to her temple and kissed her again. "Near you."

Every inch of her felt lighter, somehow, and her heart fluttered wildly in her chest. Because as strange as it seemed, she believed him. He had only just met her when they'd argued about the apartment, yet she'd felt an incredibly strong attraction to him. Was it so crazy to think he'd felt the same?

She turned so their noses touched, and pressed a soft kiss on his lips. "I'll be ready."

TELLING CLAIRE HE WASN'T poor had been the first step in easing her toward the truth. Philip knew that most women, here and on Elatyria, would be thrilled to find out their supposedly penniless suitor had wealth beyond their imagining. But Claire wasn't like most women, which was why he'd fallen in love with her. She wouldn't be happy that he'd deceived her—like the woman in the film his friends had watched last night. He only hoped she understood when he told her the whole story.

In the meantime, though, now that he was free to use some of his money, he intended to make the most of it. Claire had worked hard every single day since he'd met her, with very little help. She deserved a fantasy night out, and he intended to give it to her.

He knocked on her door right on time, heard her call from within. "Come on in, it's unlocked."

Unlocked. That displeased him, although he couldn't tell her so without revealing that he, Shelby and Teeny had been guarding her full-time again. Stating that fact might not be so bad. Telling her it was because her brother, who hadn't even contacted her in the weeks since he'd used and exploited her, was possibly in trouble again, could make things very painful for her. And causing her pain was something Philip did not intend to do. Now, or ever.

He twisted the knob and let himself in. Claire's apartment was as immaculate and prettily decorated as her shop—nothing like the units upstairs. The front room was expansive, with tasteful furniture and soft lighting. The colors suited her—cream and mauve, subdued, elegant and graceful. He suspected this was her retreat after long days in the hectic shop, which had appeared to be empty of customers only during the brief minutes he'd spent with her this morning.

Of course, that had been because Teeny had been standing right outside the door, telling customers they had to wait a few minutes.

The rest of the day had flown by; Philip had watched from the restaurant across the street as the crowds streamed

in. Knowing she was surrounded by people, he'd finally allowed himself to go upstairs and get ready for their evening.

"Sorry to keep you waiting," she said, sounding breath-
less as she emerged from a back room.

He sucked in a breath himself, his whole body heating up
as he beheld her. Claire was always lovely. Right now, though,
she was the most stunning creature he had ever seen.

She wore a black dress that clung to her curvaceous form.
It was short, coming to just above her knees, showing off her
slim legs to advantage. The dress plunged low in the front to
reveal those magnificent breasts he'd so thoroughly enjoyed
tasting. When she turned slightly to retrieve her coat, and he
saw that the back plunged even farther, he had to swallow,
hard, and remind himself to breathe.

"Are you sure you won't be too cold?" he choked out, both
loving the way she looked and dreading any other man seeing her that way.

Her eyes sparkled and her lips twitched. "I'll be fine."

She sauntered closer, her pose casual, but her trembling
mouth betraying her. She liked this power, was reveling in
her feminine strengths, confident and stunning.

Philip strode to her and grabbed her in his arms, pulling
her against him and capturing her mouth in a kiss. Their
tongues swirled, hot and hard, and he knew she'd worn this
dress on purpose, wanting to inflame him, wanting him hungry for her every minute until they finally consummated
their union.

"You know what you do to me," he growled against her
mouth.

She looked up at him, smoothing her hand over the shoulder of the tailored tuxedo he'd purchased earlier in the week.
"The same thing you do to me?"

"I hope so."

"Philip, if you told me you'd changed your mind and

wanted to walk right back to my bedroom and strip me out of this dress, I would have absolutely no objection."

That was so very tempting. But tonight wasn't about merely seducing her body. He wanted her mind, her heart, her soul.

"You will tempt me all night long," he told her as he reached for her coat and helped her put it on.

She looked the tiniest bit disappointed. So right before he led her out of the apartment, he bent to whisper, "Before we go, though, I must know.... What are you wearing under that dress?"

She licked her lips, smiling mysteriously. Then, without a word, she reached into the small black purse, opened it and withdrew a tiny tuft of soft black fabric.

"I *was* wearing these."

Gods, the woman tormented him. He grabbed the tiny panties from her hand, brought them to his mouth and rubbed the fabric against his lips, catching the warm, sweet scent of her. Then he tucked them into his pocket, planning to keep this souvenir forever.

They had to leave now or they wouldn't leave at all. He took her arm and escorted her down the hallway to the front exit. Standing outside at the curb was the long black vehicle he'd engaged for the evening.

When he led her toward it, she gasped. "You hired a limo?"

He shrugged. "I don't have a driving license."

"Ever heard of a cab?"

"This seemed a better choice."

She let him help her in, and scooted over so he could move into place beside her. Exchanging nods with the driver, who had received his instructions earlier, Philip watched as the privacy panel slid up, leaving him and Claire entirely alone and shielded from the outside world in the shadowy darkness of the car.

"This is amazing," she said as she examined the interior.

When she saw the bottle of champagne chilling in an ice bucket, with two accompanying glasses, she licked her lips. Beside it were two china plates, silverware and tempting appetizers. "You really thought of everything."

"I wanted to pamper you. To take care of you for a change."

She blinked rapidly, as if moisture threatened to spill from her eyes. "Nobody's ever done that for me before."

"Never?"

She shook her head. "Not since I was young. My mother was…not strong."

That surprised him, given the extraordinary strength and will Claire possessed. His own mother was as gracious and kind as could be, but had an iron spine. He had little use for weak women.

"My father doted on her, but then he was gone, and it was just me, her and Freddy."

"And you took over?"

"Yes."

Claire told him more, revealing so much of herself as she talked about her childhood. Many of her tales made him laugh, others had him tensing his fists, ready to hurt someone. How a father could allow himself to become addicted to games of chance, leaving his family nearly penniless, was unfathomable. How a mother could collapse into weakness under the guise of her artistic temperament, allowing her teenaged daughter to support her, was infuriating.

Yet how Claire had done it—and succeeded beyond anyone's dreams—was inspiring.

Philip had instructed the driver to cruise around the city for a while, but once the champagne and caviar were gone, he pressed a button to signal they were ready to proceed to their eventual destination. When they arrived, and the driver opened the door, Claire looked past him to the entrance for the hotel and gasped.

"This is…oh, my God, Philip, this is the Four Seasons."

"Yes, I know. The guidebook spoke highly of it."

She clutched his arm. "You can't possibly afford this."

"For one night—for *this* night—I can absolutely afford this."

She opened her mouth as if to object again, but he kissed away her words. By the time he'd finished exploring her luscious mouth, any arguments had left her mind, and she smiled as she exited the car.

Having called ahead to make arrangements, and gotten the information he needed, Philip didn't hesitate once inside. He crossed the marble-floored lobby, which was almost as graceful and elegant as his own palace, though much more crowded, and went straight to the restaurant. After he gave his name, they were led to a private table, small and intimate, in a shadowy corner.

"This is too much," Claire said as Philip helped her into her seat.

"Pampering. Remember?"

"I know, but…"

"Are you having a good time?"

"Yes, but…"

"Then please just enjoy yourself. Stop worrying, stop analyzing, stop thinking."

She hesitated, then finally nodded. "If you're sure."

"I'm quite sure."

That seemed to put an end to her worries, because for the next few hours, over what even Shelby would concede was an excellent meal, Claire was as relaxed and happy as he'd ever seen her. They talked about everything. More about her childhood, and as much as he could tell her about his.

He was finally able to admit that he was the only son of very wealthy parents, and revealed much about his daily life. She enjoyed hearing about his family. She especially liked his stories about his spoiled cousin, Shelby, who, she forced him to admit, hadn't really wanted to work in her shop tonight, and had done it only under duress.

"It sounds so wonderful, where you live," she said, after they were finishing off a dessert that couldn't begin to compare to the one they'd had the previous night. "I'd love to see it."

"You will."

She shifted a little and looked away. "I didn't mean that the way it sounded. I wasn't angling for an invitation."

"You have one."

She nodded in thanks. "I just meant I've never really been anywhere but here. My mother used to talk about her life in the ballet, before she met and married my father. She traveled all over the world, saw exotic places—glamorous cities, big castles, jungles, deserts."

His own kingdom could provide many of those things. If he wasn't mistaken, there was a jungle not too far away.

So far, so good, as they said.

"I thought you liked living here," he murmured, wanting to discover just how attached she was to her homeland.

She shrugged. "I do. But I don't know whether it's because I really like it or because I have no other options."

"You could go anywhere you want."

"Not easily," she said with a sigh.

"Because of your shop?"

"The shop was a means to an end. A way to support myself and my brother. I never finished college, and neither did he. I inherited the building and thought about selling it."

Would Philip never have met her in that case? It didn't bear thinking about. "Why did you decide not to?" he asked, suspecting he knew the reason. Claire wasn't one to take the easy road.

"I suppose because I was thinking long-term, not short-term. I had enough money to get by and to do something with the building. I don't have many other skills, other than being able to make the most fattening foods on the planet."

"Delectable," he murmured, thinking about some of the specialties he'd sampled. None compared to her, but they were all better than any sweets he'd tasted in any world.

"It seemed going into business would be better than getting a big chunk of cash, which my brother could try to squeeze out of me in dribs and drabs."

Philip's hand tightened in his lap as he thought about her brother. "Have you heard from him?" he was compelled to ask.

A shadow crossed her face. "No, not a word in weeks."

"And you're worried?"

"Yes, plus more than a little hurt, to be honest. I was furious at first. Now I just feel betrayed."

Philip reached out and grasped her hand. "I am going to be thankful every day for the rest of my life that your wastrel brother took advantage of us both."

She gazed at him, her lovely eyes gleaming in the candlelight. "I suspect I am, too," she whispered.

They stared at one another for a long moment, saying so many things without speaking. And at that moment, Philip knew Claire was in love with him, too. Neither of them had said the words, but the emotion was there, thick and powerful, swirling between them like an undeniable force.

"Philip?"

"Yes, love?"

"I think I'm ready for you to take me home now."

He smiled, knowing what she wanted. She was as ready to make love as he was. What she didn't realize was that they didn't have a long car ride between them and ultimate pleasure.

"Let's go," he told her, reaching out once more for her hand.

She glanced around, looking for their waiter. "Is this how you could afford to take me here?" she asked with a chuckle. "Are we doing a dine and dash?"

"Not at all. Everything's taken care of already. They'll bill the meal to my room."

Surprise and excitement flashed in her eyes. "You mean we don't have to ride all the way back to my place?"

"No, Claire. We just have to ride up in an elevator to our suite." He slid an arm around her waist. "I'm not letting you get away from me until morning."

THEY DIDN'T EXCHANGE a word as they left the restaurant and crossed the lobby to the elevators. The sexual tension that had been building between them for days was about to erupt. She kept herself in check, not touching him, though they walked closely enough for their legs to brush. If he reached for her, or she for him, they'd be making out in the elevator, not giving a damn about who might walk in on them.

And, of course, someone did step in—an older couple and two businessmen, forcing them to the back corner. Claire wondered what they must think, given the tension between Philip and her. Musk and desire seeped from every one of Philip's masculine pores, and her own body had to be giving off all kinds of pheromones. She felt practically in heat around this man.

He nearly sent her through the roof when he reached into his pocket, retrieved the black silk panties she'd given him at the start of the evening, and brought them to his lips. To anyone looking over a shoulder, he might appear to be wiping his mouth with a black handkerchief. But Claire felt her legs sag, and had to lean against the back wall, clenching her thighs together as moisture welled from her aching sex.

For the past twenty-four hours she'd been wanting to be

filled by him. If they were alone, she'd hike up her dress and take him right now, mirrors and cameras be damned.

She only hoped he'd brought that entire box of condoms, because she intended for tonight to be one she would never forget.

Theirs was the first stop, thank goodness, and Philip twined his fingers in hers and pulled her after him the moment the doors swished open. Claire caught the stare of the one woman in the group and would swear the older lady, who looked long-married and content, gave her a surreptitious wink.

A few steps, the flash of an electronic key and they were inside an opulent room. But Claire wasn't even curious enough to look around. She just wanted *him*.

He seemed every bit as frenzied. The moment the door clicked shut behind them, he bent and picked her up in his arms, carrying her across the huge suite to the massive bed that dominated the bedroom. The covers were already pulled down and, she was shocked to see, red rose petals were strewn over the silky sheets.

"You arranged all this?"

"Of course," he said, as he lowered her onto the bed and followed her down.

"Thank you," she whispered, looping her arms around his neck and pulling him down for a sultry kiss.

Their tongues thrust lazily and the kiss went on and on. They shared each breath, and their bodies melted together, angles welcoming curves. Philip never moved his mouth from hers as he began to touch her, stroking her arms, her neck, her throat, her hair. When his fingertips brushed the top curves of her breasts, she arched toward him, ready for him to intensify his caresses.

Instead of ending the kiss so she could unzip her dress and pull it down, he kept his mouth on hers and slid his hand farther, past her stomach, her hip, her thighs. Until he reached the hem and began to tug it up.

She quivered, anticipation making her hold her breath as his fingers worked her nerve endings. Her legs were shaking before he was anywhere near their apex, and when he finally did reach the curls covering her sex, she cried out against his mouth.

"Do you know how much I loved tasting this?" he asked, finally pulling away to kiss her jaw, her neck, her ear.

"As much as I loved tasting you?"

"More," he insisted, finally reaching around to unfasten her dress. She sat up a little, helping him, watching his eyes grow nearly black as he uncovered her body. The dress had a built-in bra, since it was so low-cut in the back, and when he realized she wasn't wearing a stitch underneath, he growled in approval.

"I want to feel you pressed against me," she said, pushing his jacket off his shoulders. "Every inch of you."

He got up from off the bed, his eyes never leaving her face as he stripped out of his clothes. Claire lay there watching him drop the jacket, the tie, the shirt. When he reached for his trousers she nibbled her lip, eager to see him naked.

Of course, she wasn't totally naked herself; she was still wearing a pair of black, spike-heeled shoes. When she reached down to unbuckle them, he shook his head slowly, suggestively.

She left them on.

"I've never seen a more perfectly built man," she admitted, her eyes devouring him as he unbuttoned his fly. He was gorgeous, all broad and lean and sculpted.

The trousers fell, as did his boxer briefs, and she swallowed hard. Seeing that huge erection reminded her of how he'd tasted, how just the thick tip of it had filled her mouth.

She didn't have any worries about taking him into her

body now—first, because she wanted him desperately and was more wet and aroused than she'd ever been in her life. Second, because she knew that, no matter what, he would take care of her.

As if reading her mind, he reached for her and cupped her cheek. "I'll never hurt you."

She extended her arms, pulling him down to her. "I know."

They began kissing again, and this time, with the press of their naked bodies—her bare leg slipping between his, her breasts crushed against his chest—she groaned at the rightness of it.

"Please, Philip," she whispered as he kissed his way down her neck, "don't make me wait. I've been waiting long enough."

He knew what she meant, and reached for his pants. "I packed us a small bag," he admitted. "The rest of the condoms are in it. But in case we didn't make it here, I tucked one in my pocket."

"Smart boy," she said, laughing softly.

She watched greedily as he tore open the packet and slipped the condom over his rigid cock, noting that his hands shook the tiniest bit, as if he was just as affected by the importance of this moment as she was.

It was important. Vitally so. Because for the first time in her life, she was about to make love with a man she loved.

She'd never been in love before, never experienced anything like this, but Claire had no doubt that's what she felt for Philip.

"Now, please," she begged, spreading her legs, arching up to welcome him.

He settled himself between her thighs and she wrapped her ankles around his hips, pulling him closer. Wonderfully restrained, Philip gently nudged into her channel, giving her time to adjust to him. He groaned when he found her hot, wet and ready for him, and began to sink deeper.

"Oh, yes," she whispered as he filled her, making a place for himself in her body the way he had in her heart. She tangled her fingers in his hair, pressing kisses against his throat and chest, wanting to wrap herself around him and never let go. "Fill me up, Philip, so I'll always remember what it's like to have you as a part of me."

"Oh, Claire, you always will," he promised as he bent to kiss her. Their mouths locked as he plunged deep, filling her so thoroughly, so perfectly, she wondered how she'd ever lived this many years without realizing she'd been incomplete.

They began to move, first with slow, gentle thrusts, then with harder, more intense ones. Every stroke was both a question and a promise, every touch had many meanings, every kiss was like a vow. At one point, Claire rolled him over and climbed on top, wanting to look down at him, to see him helpless with desire for her. He gave her all she wanted and more, gazing up at her adoringly.

She didn't know how long it went on, just knew that they made love for what seemed like hours, until he'd become so much a part of her she didn't think she was ever going to be able to let him go.

She climaxed again and again, each time more intense and blissful than the last. When he finally came, he whispered the sweetest words against her mouth.

"I love you, Claire."

And she could say absolutely nothing but the same.

"I love you, too."

7

THE NEXT TEN DAYS passed in a blur and were among the happiest of Philip's life.

Since their night at the hotel, he and Claire were inseparable. He slept with her in her bed each night and awakened to her smiling face every morning. Several times a day he found an excuse to end up in the kitchen of her shop, sometimes just watching her whip up some fantastical treat that would delight a child on Christmas morning. Sometimes helping her by unloading boxes, cleaning bowls or even stirring batters.

He even, as he'd threatened, got Teeny to help. When it became obvious that Claire's business had become popular, and that she wasn't getting much rest, he made sure his friends lent a hand wherever possible. To his shock—and Claire's amusement—his bodyguard had a keen eye and a steady hand, and took real delight in creating intricate flowers made of icing, or delicate cakes.

It was now just a few days before Christmas. Just a few days before he needed to leave for home. While he and Claire had talked about tomorrow and the month after and the year after that as if they would still be together, he had not yet asked her to be his wife.

He couldn't, not until he told her who he really was and

where he was from. Philip only hoped that when he did, she wouldn't decide she wanted nothing to do with a world she might consider backward, since it lacked many of the amenities of hers. Of course, it had its own delights, and so much beauty, but until she experienced it for herself she might not realize just how magical it could be.

They had just finished decorating a small tree in Claire's living room. He suspected she'd been putting it off in hope that she would see or hear from her brother, as the tradition had been one she'd shared with him in recent years. So Philip did all he could to make the evening a memorable one, wanting her to have new, good memories to replace those that made her sad.

They'd listened to jolly music, shared ginger-flavored cookies, and laughed together as he tried to figure out how to hang a blasted strand of tiny lights. Frankly, he preferred candles, but she insisted that would be a fire hazard. The two of them finally ended up curled together on the floor in front of the tree, looking at the light reflecting off the beautiful red ornaments as a long, silent night descended.

"Ready for bed?" he asked, kissing her temple.

"Yes, except I just realized how fabulous those ginger cookies were, and decided I'm going to make some for the shop tomorrow," she said with a light laugh.

"Huh, always thinking of your work," he teased.

She tickled his ribs, rolling over and getting to her feet. "Go on to bed. I'll be right behind you. I just want to run back to the kitchen to see if I'm going to have everything I need, or if I'll have to go out to the restaurant supply place in the morning before we open to pick up more cookie cutters."

He frowned as he stood up. "I'll accompany you."

Rolling her eyes, she pushed him toward the bedroom. "Don't be ridiculous, it's twenty feet away. Go get the bed warm and ready for me."

Thinking of all the things he could do to be ready for her, he leered. "As you wish."

She was giggling as she left, and he went into the bathroom to wash the sap from the tree off his hands. He intended to touch her everywhere tonight, and wouldn't want to get that piney goo anywhere it wouldn't easily wash off.

Heading to the bedroom, he glanced at the clock and realized it had been at least ten minutes since she'd left—more than long enough for her to check on some cookie cutters. A hint of tension crawled up his spine. Though he'd been with her every day and had seen no sign of trouble, Philip couldn't help worrying.

Deciding to check on her, he left her apartment and walked down the hallway toward the shop.

He was a few feet from the door when he heard a man's voice.

"Listen, lady, if you know what's good for you, you'll sign. My boss is offering you one last chance. You sell him the building at a fair price, and he throws in your brother's markers to sweeten the deal."

Philip's whole body stiffened at the gruff, threatening tone, not to mention the words. Anger roared through him, and not even considering taking the time to go upstairs and get Teeny, he flung the door open and burst into the kitchen. Casting a quick glance around, he saw Freddy Hoffman standing by the sink, his shoulders slumped, his expression stressed and unhappy.

Claire was near the counter, a shaking hand over her mouth. Next to her stood a scar-faced, burly man who towered over her. He was leaning toward her in an intimidating way, and growled like a thwarted bull when Philip appeared. As if knowing Claire was about to run to him, the man grabbed her by the arm, his grip punishing.

Rage took over. With a cry of pure fury, Philip tore across

the floor in two long strides, lashing out and striking the man's jaw. The thug stumbled back, releasing his grip on Claire, who went spinning. Seeing that she was all right, Philip focused entirely on the ugly stranger, who was curling up his fists for a brawl.

Philip hadn't trained with the best fighters in Elatyria for nothing. He was the head of his country's army, had fought nomadic warriors and thieves and pugilists. He knew how to handle himself.

"Philip, watch out!" Claire cried from the corner.

He ignored her, leaning forward defensively as the hulk came swinging. One uppercut to the jaw, a hard left to the midsection and a final right in the kidneys and the other man went down.

"Crawl out of here right now, scum, and don't ever come back," Philip snarled at the man, who was hunched over in pain.

"You don't know who you're messin' with, or who I work for! I'm tryin' to make a deal!"

"Make it with the punk who owes you money," he snapped, glaring at Freddy, who was watching wide-eyed in shock. "If you ever lay hands on this woman again, I'll make sure they don't find your body. And believe me, I know how to do it."

The rough-looking man staggered to his feet and stumbled toward the door. Before leaving, he glanced back at Freddy. "You have twenty-four hours to make good. Then you're mine."

Philip was no longer paying attention. He hurried over to Claire, who was leaning against the counter, gasping and rubbing her arm where the beast had grabbed her. Philip ran a hand over her to ensure it wasn't broken. When he'd confirmed she was more shaken up than hurt, he pulled her hard against him. "It's all right now, Claire. He won't ever bother you again."

"Philip! Oh, God, thank you for coming. I didn't even hear them until I walked in."

"You weren't supposed to be here," Freddy cried, finally rushing over to his sister. "I was planning to get him in and out without you ever knowing."

"Were you going to sell the building out from under her the way you rented the upstairs?" Philip snapped, unable to hide his disgust with the weak young man.

"No!" he said. "I just… Louie the Rat King tried so hard to get Claire to sell last month. I think that's why they kept giving me lines of credit. So I agreed to show his guy around."

"The Rat King?" she said, sounding confused. "You mean he was that investor who kept coming in here?"

Freddy nodded miserably. "I didn't know, I swear. And I was just trying to buy time, to pretend you were thinking about selling, while I figured out how to get the rest of the money."

Philip didn't know if Claire believed her brother, but wasn't nearly ready to give Freddy the benefit of the doubt himself. "What happened to the money I paid you?"

"I gave him most of it, I swear. I paid off the first debt! The extra five, well, I figured I'd try to build it back up so I could totally give Claire every penny. Only…"

"You lost it. And then some."

"Right."

"You selfish fool," Philip snapped.

Claire was openly weeping now. "How could you, Freddy? After everything we've been through? After Dad…"

"I just didn't want to be a burden on you anymore," her brother insisted. "I thought if I could make some quick money, I could take care of you for a change."

"She has me to do that now," Philip said. Claire glanced at him, visibly startled by his words. "Now, here's the bargain I will make with you," he said to Freddy. "I'll pay off your debt under one condition. You go do something useful with your life, and don't come back until you've grown up."

"Philip…"

"No, Claire. You can't keep coddling him. He has to stand on his own two feet."

"Look, I appreciate the offer, but this is our problem."

He turned to look down at her, seeing the sadness on her face. She seemed to have the weight of the world on her shoulders. "No," he told her. "It's mine, too. You're my family, Claire. I intend to marry you. That makes your brother's problem my problem."

Her jaw fell. "What on earth are you saying?"

Not the right thing, obviously. Some romantic suitor he was. The most eligible prince in the kingdoms and he'd completely mucked up the one and only marriage proposal he ever intended to make. Not only was the timing bad, given the audience and the situation, but he still hadn't told her the entire truth about himself. He would shortly, but not until he'd finished dealing with her brother.

"Are you serious? You're really going to marry my sister?" Freddy asked, sounding more interested in that part of the conversation than in the financial part. Which was one small point in his favor.

"I am."

"Do I have any say in this?" Claire asked, sounding annoyed. "Look, Philip, you can't just take over my life, make these decisions, tell me I'm marrying you and order my brother away."

"Of course I can," he replied. "You love me."

She sighed and ran a weary hand through her beautiful hair. "Yeah, okay, I do. But that doesn't mean I'm going to let you solve all my problems."

"Why not? Isn't that what people in love do?"

"No. They solve them together. They work together, make

decisions together." She glared at her brother. "Deal with ir-responsible siblings together."

"Very well, then," Philip said, "we'll do it together. As soon as we get married."

If anything, she looked even more unsure. "You can't pro-pose to me just to save my brother's ass."

"I'm not," he insisted. "I intended to ask you to marry me tomorrow, and to come away with me on Monday."

Her eyes widened in surprise, as if she didn't believe him.

"I have much to tell you, Claire," he explained, "and I will, when we're alone. But the one thing you must know, before we say another word, is that I am leaving on Christmas Eve. I have to go back to my home, which is far away from here, and I want to take you with me."

Shock made her take a step or two back, until she was leaning against the counter, eyeing him as if she'd never seen him before. Even Freddy, who'd been staying quiet, probably counting his blessings, looked stunned.

"You want to take her away? Like, forever?"

"She can come back to visit, and if you ever manage to grow up and become a responsible adult, there will always be a place for you in our home."

Hmm. Come to think of it, a good place for Freddy would be in the Kingdom's army. The idea bore considering.

Claire was shaking her head in confusion, holding a hand up as if trying to stop him from saying anything more. "You think I can just walk out the door the day after tomorrow, put my hand in yours, travel to who knows where and forget about my responsibilities? My home, my shop, my family?"

He heard the confusion in her voice, not to mention the longing. He didn't suppose this was a good time to mention she'd be leaving her entire world behind, too.

Damn Freddy and his schemes. This was not how Philip had envisioned this moment.

But time was running out, and the proposal had been made. So all he could do was slowly nod. "Yes, Claire. That's exactly what I am hoping you will do."

She stared at him, then at her brother, then at Philip again. Her eyes were luminous, wet, and her mouth was quivering. He longed to reach out and take her in his arms, to assure her all would be well, but he couldn't force her. Claire had to decide on her own if she loved him enough to take the next step.

Finally, after what seemed to him to be a lifetime, she gave him her answer.

"I'm sorry, Philip. I'm truly sorry. But the answer is no."

CHRISTMAS EVE WAS usually one of Claire's favorite days of the year. She had wonderful childhood memories of last-minute baking, wrapping and decorating, and her parents had always seemed happiest around the holidays. With her bustling, successful shop, this year should have been another really good one.

Instead, she spent much of the day dashing back into the kitchen to shed a few more tears and wipe her eyes.

The man she loved—the man of her dreams—had asked her to marry him, to go away with him, and she'd said no.

It wasn't just her refusal making her cry, it was the memory of the look on his beautiful, beloved face. Philip had appeared completely bereft and shocked. She knew he was a little spoiled, and that he came from money, so perhaps he wasn't used to not getting his own way. But deep down, she feared it was worse than that. She was afraid she'd truly broken his heart.

Well, he wasn't alone. Hers was broken, too.

"Are you okay?" Freddy asked, joining her in the back room.

She'd kicked her brother out Saturday night, a few minutes after Philip had strode from the kitchen without another word. She just hadn't been able to deal with Freddy after she'd had her heart torn in two. He had come to the shop yesterday, but she'd sent him away once more, still not ready to talk to him. He'd come back again first thing this morning, and she knew she'd wallowed long enough. It was time to start thinking clearly.

"I'll be all right," she insisted, dabbing at her eyes with her apron.

"Have you heard from him since the other night?"

She shook her head. "No. He might already be gone."

Claire blinked as tears threatened to well up once more. The thought of not seeing Philip again was enough to crush her.

It wasn't just that she loved him and wanted to be with him. She *liked* him, and he had become the most important part of her life. More important than the shop or her home, or even her brother, whom she'd looked after for so long. Philip had become everything. And she'd let him walk away.

"So why don't you go to him?"

"And say what? Sorry I stomped on your offer—want a cup of coffee?"

"How about 'Sorry I said no, you caught me off guard, I love you and want to marry you'?"

That sounded lovely. And impossible. "I can't."

Freddy blew out a disbelieving breath. "Why not?"

"I can't just leave."

"I repeat—why not? It's not like you love this place. You and I both know you started it because you needed to keep my greedy fingers off your money."

"True."

Her brother dropped his head, looking sheepish. "The point is, Claire, I've been watching you for a few weeks now."

"What the hell is it with men feeling the need to watch me?"

"I was ashamed to come back," he admitted, sounding

truly contrite. "And I was afraid Louie the Rat King would send his goons over to bother you, so I stuck around the neighborhood. I did see one of 'em a couple weeks ago, and stopped him from coming any closer."

"Oh, Freddy, what a mess."

"But it's my mess. Not yours. Your life could be great. I've seen the way you are with Philip. And I've definitely seen the way he is with you. That dude is madly in love with you, Claire."

"Madly? Maybe. But am I *mad* enough to just walk away from my entire life and go off with him to who knows where? He says he's from Spain, but I've never heard him speak a word of Spanish. For all I know he lives in the back of beyond!"

Her brother shrugged. "So what? Does it really matter where you live if you honestly love each other?"

She stared at him, wondering when on earth he'd started to sound like a genuine grown-up. Freddy had always been the one needing advice. He'd sure never offered it. But now he was making a lot of sense.

"You really think I could just walk away?"

"Not only do I think you could, I think you should," he replied. "And it has nothing to do with my problems or him bailing me out."

Though she imagined he was considering that a nice bonus. Ah well, leopards couldn't change their spots overnight.

"What about the shop?"

"That lady you hired to work in the back is pretty amazing. I bet she could manage the place. Hell, I'll stay here and help her."

Gaping, Claire could only laugh.

"I'm serious. You can get your accountant to handle the money side if you don't trust me. Between me, Mrs. West and Jeannie, we'll do all right." Freddy came close and took

Claire's hand, staring her in the eye, not once shifting his gaze. "I swear to you, I've learned my lesson. I want to help you. I want your dreams to come true, since you've sacrificed so many of them for my sake. Please, Claire…. You have the chance for real happiness. Grab it."

Could she really? Was there still a chance?

Her heart was thudding in her chest, and every instinct urged her to do what her brother said. To grab happiness and live life to the fullest, with no regrets, no recriminations.

Philip was the man she wanted to spend her life with. And she intended to tell him that.

She only hoped she wasn't too late.

PHILIP DECIDED TO HEAD for home without saying goodbye to Claire. He simply couldn't see her again, knowing he'd lost her.

Not when there was something he could do about changing that.

Saturday night, when he'd come upstairs dejected and defeated, Shelby had insisted that he would find someone else. As if anyone would ever make Philip's heart beat fast in his chest again. He was thirty years old, had been looking for the right woman since he was sixteen, and had never even come close until he'd met Claire Hoffman.

It was her or it was no one.

Teeny had urged him to not give up, to go right back downstairs and get her to change her mind. But neither he nor Shelby had seen what had happened. The way Philip had bared his heart to her…the way she'd rejected it.

She might love him, but she wasn't ready for a life with him. Which meant he needed more time. The only way he could get it was to go home, tell his parents the truth about what had happened, and ask them to release him from his promise. Ask them to give him a little more time to win the woman he wanted.

"They'll agree. They have to," he told himself as he looked out the window of the train at the passing countryside.

When he'd come to America several weeks ago, he had arrived through one of the crossings into Europe, and had flown over the great sea. But this world was bigger than his own. He could travel faster—cover more distance—in Elatyria. So even though he would have to take a ship over the much smaller ocean there, he intended to cross between worlds here, in America, by way of the nearest major border. Hopefully, he would be back in his own kingdom by week's end.

He had left Teeny and Shelby in New York, both because he fully intended to come back, and because he wanted them to protect Claire while the threat of her brother's creditors hung over her. Considering he'd left Shelby with enough money to pay off the bookie, that threat shouldn't last for long. However, Philip didn't trust the man he'd fought with not to seek revenge on him, and take it out on Claire.

The sooner Philip got back to New York—back to her— the better.

He reached the nearest major crossing, which was just outside a town they called Boston, by late in the afternoon. He had hired a car to take him to the precise coordinates, shrugging off the driver's curious look as he dropped him along a country road. Waiting until the man and his vehicle were well out of sight, Philip made his way toward a long, low field, to the invisible border that existed in a small stand of trees on the far side of it. Just a few more steps and he would be back on his own world, where he belonged, even though he would be leaving a huge part of himself—his heart—behind.

Already rehearsing what he would say to his parents when he saw them, he wondered about Claire, what she was doing, what she would think of his departure. He felt so close to her, it was as if he could hear her voice.

"Philip, wait!"

He froze. That hadn't been a waking dream or a fantasy. That had been the voice of the woman he loved.

He spun around, not sure he could believe his ears. When he saw Claire leaping out of a yellow taxi, with a smiling Shelby and Teeny right behind her, he nearly dropped to his knees in relief.

She ran to him. Philip shook off his shocked immobility and strode to meet her. Swinging her up in his arms, he pressed kiss after kiss on her face, too happy to see her to even ask how this had come to be. He held her as if he would never let her go. He never *would* let her go from his heart, and definitely didn't intend to let her out of his arms or sight for a very long time.

"Claire, what are you doing here?"

"I had to wish you a Merry Christmas, didn't I?"

"And a Merry Christmas to you, my love," he whispered, kissing her temple, breathing her in, wanting to imprint her scent and her memory on every part of him.

"You asked me to come with you," she said, looking up at him in reproach. "Then, you big jerk, you left without saying goodbye?"

"But…but—"

"A woman's entitled to change her mind, isn't she?"

"Oh, my love, of course she is." He kissed her again, softly, gently, wondering if there would ever be a moment in his life as perfect as this one.

Yes, it was cold and they were in the middle of nowhere. Yes, he was in a strange land, far from all he knew. But it was still magical. Almost as magical as his home, which would be ever so much more so now that she would share it with him.

They stood wrapped in each other's embrace for several

long moments, their hearts pounding in unison. A soft snow began to fall. It hadn't snowed much during his time in New York, and never when he was with Claire, and he found he liked standing in it with her. The delicate flakes kissed his cheeks and came to rest on her beautiful hair.

He owed her a better proposal. "I love you, Claire. Will you be my wife? My princess?" he murmured, his face pressed against hers.

"Oh, yes," she replied, hugging him tighter. Then, as if she suddenly thought about what he'd said, she stiffened and looked up at him. "Princess?"

He cleared his throat, eyeing Teeny and Shelby, who strode up to them, carrying their bags and an extra one that must belong to her.

"You didn't tell her?"

"Thought we'd leave that one to you," said his cousin with a smirk.

"Tell me what?"

Philip thought about it, considered what to say.

Then he realized there was a much better way. They were steps away from the border, and seeing something was better than hearing about it any day.

He gazed into her eyes. "Do you trust me?"

"With my life."

Her faith in him was humbling, though he knew that she *could* trust him with her life. He would never let anything or anyone hurt her, and would gladly die to keep her safe.

"And would you want to be with me no matter where we go or what we do?"

Her expression was tender, so sweet, loving and sincere. "I do, Philip. For richer or poorer, in sickness and in health… bring it on. Bring it all on."

He loved the certainty in her voice, and the glimmer of excitement in her eyes.

"How about, uh, no electricity?"

Her mouth rounded, but he kissed away any words she might have spoken. By the time they broke apart, she was smiling broadly.

"Whatever," she whispered. "Let's do this."

So, taking her arm in his, he turned to face the small stand of trees and the shimmering veil he could just make out through the drifting snow. They walked toward it, and though he wasn't escorting her down the aisle after saying their official vows, this moment felt a little like he suspected that one would.

"What *is* this place?" she asked, squinting, obviously seeing something in the air, or even feeling the aura that existed in this thin veil between worlds.

"Close your eyes," he told her, keeping her hand tightly entwined with his. "It might seem like a dream, but you'll be safe, and I'll explain everything momentarily."

"Philip?" she said, a little uncertain.

"I love you, Claire. I promise you we'll be together, and I'll make you happy every day for as long as you live."

She nodded up at him, any reservations gone, her decision made. And together, arm in arm, they stepped through the veil, across the border and into an entirely different world.

Epilogue

AND SO THE handsome prince returned home to his palace, bringing with him a beautiful maiden, whom he'd chosen to be his bride. There was much sadness among the ladies of the kingdoms, who had vied for his hand, but in his own palace, and among his own people and family members, happiness abounded.

The new princess was the delight of the court, the apple of her father-in-law's eye, a close friend and confidante to the queen, and above all, a loving and adoring wife to her husband. Everyone who visited the couple, and their growing family, commented on the obvious devotion between the two, admitting that the royals were indeed wise to marry for love rather than duty.

The princess won over even her most jealous detractors with her beauty, strength and kindness…not to mention her delicious candies, which became renowned throughout the land. Every so often, she and the prince would disappear, going to visit her family back home—some said she had a handsome brother who was a prince of industry in his land. Whenever she was asked about her background and where she came from, all she would say was that she'd come from a cold place faraway, and had never truly known warmth and bliss until her beloved prince had come into her life and swept her off her feet.

And together, Claire and her prince lived happily ever after.

* * * * *

JENNIFER LaBRECQUE

MY TRUE LOVE GAVE TO ME...

Prologue

GERTRUDE "Trudie" Brown's heart felt as if it was breaking right in two. It was almost a physical pain. Her best friend Knox Whitaker was disappearing right before her eyes, becoming someone she didn't know...and someone she wasn't sure she particularly liked.

She brushed away the bugs that came with July in Alaska and shifted on the rock beside Knox. Jessup, Knox's dog, half white German shepherd and half bull terrier and 100 percent sweetheart, tucked his paws more firmly beneath his chest and put his head down. He obviously sensed the strain between Trudie and Knox. She knew how the dog felt. Not even the splendor of the impending midnight sunset over Anchorage—the golden horizon rich with red-and-pink-hued clouds—soothed her spirit.

Knox ran his hands over his hair, the gesture weary. "Take whatever you want out of the house," Knox said. "The agents are coming in and opening the place for an estate sale on Friday. The rest will be hauled to the dump."

Trudie felt sick. "Estate sale? The dump?" No! He couldn't mean it. "How can you even consider letting strangers traipse in and out, picking through the minutiae of Mormor's life, the things she held dear, and then discard the rest?"

She had been seven, Knox eight, when he came to live with his grandmother next door to Trudie and her parents. Nineteen years ago Trudie's heart had wept for the orphaned boy, his blue eyes somber with grief and wariness from his parents' deaths in a car crash. It was as if her heart had linked with his to help him heal. They'd grown up together. They'd grown together.

She'd had girlfriends and dated an array of guys, but she couldn't recall a time since that fateful day he'd arrived here that they hadn't been best friends. Even when he'd left to do his undergrad work at University of Alaska in Fairbanks and then gone on to vet school at Washington State University while Trudie had remained in Anchorage, they'd stayed close. When he returned home and joined a small practice, he and Trudie had met once a week for dinner to catch up.

And then Mormor had died.

The last three months had been terrible. Mormor had gone quickly, which was exactly how she would've wanted it.

Even after he'd left for college, Knox had called his grandmother every week to check on her and when he'd returned to Anchorage, he'd been diligent in keeping tabs on her. In the last year, as her mobility decreased, the weekly calls had become daily ones. So, when Mormor hadn't answered one morning, Knox had left his practice and gone to her house to check on her. He'd called Trudie on his way. It would turn out to be the last "real" conversation he and Trudie had.

When Knox arrived, Mormor was dead. He'd found her sitting in her recliner, a word search puzzle on her lap, her cat Tonto curled up beside her cold form. Trudie's mom had gone next door when she'd seen Knox's truck. She said Mormor looked peaceful, as if she'd simply drifted off to sleep.

As death went, everyone agreed Mormor's had been good. The woman had valued her independence and never wanted to be a burden. She'd always said that a quick exit beat a slow decline. So, from that perspective she'd been granted her wish. But the loss was…well, it was dreadful.

While Knox agreed her death was exactly what Mormor would've wanted, he'd become remote and withdrawn. He was distant with Trudie. Her mom had reassured her, it was simply part of the grief process, but it was confusing for Trudie.

Although she had moved into her own apartment years ago, when she visited her folks, she always dropped by to visit Mormor, even if it was only for a minute. Mormor had been like a surrogate grandmother to her.

Trudie missed her, too, but she wasn't dealing with it by pushing Knox away. He was the one who had bailed on their weekly dinner for the last month. It didn't make any sense to her. Over the years she and Knox had talked about everything, but since Mormor's death he wouldn't talk to her about anything.

And now this? He was opening his grandmother's house to strangers and selling it? Granted, she didn't quite know what she'd expected him to do—he had his own place near his vet clinic, but she'd thought perhaps he'd hold onto the house or maybe move in. It seemed so cold and callous to just sell a house that held so many memories. She didn't get it. At this point, she didn't understand, but how could she when he wouldn't talk to her. This was the longest conversation they'd had in weeks, and quite frankly she'd been surprised and excited when he'd suggested they meet for one of their late-night hikes, which had become a rarity rather than a regular event.

Knox shrugged his broad shoulders but didn't look at her. The sun, quickly sinking toward the horizon, threw his beloved features into relief—the straight, strong nose, the firm jaw and square chin, the slight curl to his hair where it lay against his neck. "Elsa says it's the best way to handle it. She says it's all junk and she's right."

Trudie's hand itched. She didn't know who she wanted to

slap more or harder—Knox or the beautiful Elsa Borjeson. Elsa and Knox had met a couple of months ago when she'd rear-ended him at a traffic light. Over the years, Knox and Trudie had dated people that the other one wasn't so wild about. Come to think of it, they'd never particularly liked each other's choices. However, there was something particularly offputting about Elsa.... Mormor hadn't liked the cool blonde either.

"Since when did your grandmother's life and her things become junk?" Trudie asked through gritted teeth.

He at least had the grace to look ashamed. Elsa's influence hadn't totally erased all traces of her friend...yet. "Well, Mormor's stuff isn't exactly junk." He shifted on the rock and his shoulders stiffened. "But she's gone and it's time to move on."

That didn't even sound like Knox. He might as well be reading from a script penned by Elsa. Trudie wrapped her arms around her bent legs and rested her head on her knees, studying him as the light bathed him in a golden glow.

He glanced at her, inquiry in his denim-blue eyes at her silence. "What?"

An ineffable sadness filled her. "What's happened to you?" she said softly. Her words seemed to float on the breeze that riffled her hair against her face. "I don't know you anymore."

It was a whisper, more of an aside to herself, yet he heard her.

A remoteness shadowed his eyes, rendering him inaccessible to her in a way he'd never been before. "I grew up, Trudie. Maybe it's time that you did as well."

The harshness of his words made her wince. Although his physical features were familiar, his heart was not the same. She loved him, but she couldn't, at this moment, say she liked him. So, if this was his version of growing up and he wanted her to join him on this path...well, no thanks.

"Not if it means becoming what you've become."

He looked away from her. "If that's the way you feel."

Trudie wished she could snap him out of whatever mind set he had slipped into. While she knew everyone in life was responsible for themselves, it was as if Elsa had Knox under a spell, as if she'd smudged all the good things, clouding the way he saw the world. It wasn't particularly fair to lay the blame all on Elsa, but the more time Knox spent with the woman, the darker his outlook became, the more cynical, and the more distant he grew.

Trudie had never censored herself with Knox and she didn't plan to start now. "Yeah, that's exactly how I feel. I don't want to get to the point where I consider my past junk."

"That's just as well," Knox said. "Our relationship makes Elsa a little uncomfortable so maybe it's best if we take a break from one another."

Elsa uncomfortable... Take a break.... Surely Trudie had heard him wrong. "What?" Their respective dates had never gotten in the way of them—Trudie and Knox—before.

"Elsa doesn't really understand our relationship. I've tried explaining that you and I are just friends, buddies, sort of the same as me and Danny, but she doesn't get it. It makes her uneasy when I'm with you."

"So, you're telling me you don't want to spend time with me because your girlfriend doesn't like me?"

Push had come to shove a couple of times before. David Peters, her senior prom date, hadn't liked Knox. She'd dumped David. Missy Fairington, one of Knox's girlfriends, was bitchy about Trudie. Missy had become history pretty quickly. Trudie and Knox's friendship had always superseded other relationships...until now.

"It's not so much that she doesn't like you—"

"Don't insult me by lying to me."

"She doesn't get you. She doesn't get our relationship.

She doesn't understand that you and I can just be friends and that's all there is to it."

If a woman was going to break up their friendship, it could've at least been someone who would love him, care for him, bring out the best in him—someone who would make him happy. That, Trudie could swallow. But, Elsa was doing none of that.

She drew a deep breath, and then laid it on the line. "Knox, I don't think she's good for you."

"She said you were jealous of her."

Trudie had already searched her soul. She wasn't jealous of Elsa, although the other woman was beautiful and obviously Knox was smitten. Trudie didn't like her because, plain and simple, Elsa wasn't a nice person. She was cold, calculating and manipulative…and it was insane that Knox couldn't see it. Love must have truly blinded him.

She didn't know what had happened to her friend, but even worse, there wasn't a thing she could do about it. Mormor had always said everyone had to choose and walk their own path. Tears burned at the back of her throat. She swallowed hard.

"I'm not jealous of Elsa," she said, her voice calm and flat.

He ignored her comment. "I'll call you in a couple of weeks after the dust settles."

He wouldn't call because there was no dust to settle. There was only Elsa.

The sun, in one powerful final illumination before it retired for the evening, cast him in a golden glow, and in that moment, her entire world shifted. She loved him. She'd always loved him, but this was different. She loved him in the way a woman loves a man, a partner. She was in love with him. It was as if she had to lose him to discover the truth of what he was to her.

The realization shook her. Shattered her. Left her uncertain. Trudie stood, her legs not quite steady beneath her. She placed her hands lightly on his broad shoulders, resisting the urge to curl her fingers into his solidness, his warmth. She leaned down and pressed a kiss against his temple, his scent enveloping her, her cheek brushing against his hair.

He was so dear to her.

Knox caught her fingers in his. "I'll call," he said, repeating his earlier…assertion…vow…platitude…. No, he wouldn't. "You're okay, right?" No, she wasn't okay and she wasn't sure that she ever would be without him. She wavered, almost blurting her discovery, but it would just be awkward. He was all hung up on Elsa so what was the point in baring her soul?

She tugged her hand free. "I'm fine."

Trudie bent and scratched Jessup behind the ears. His gaze was nothing short of woeful as he looked up at her. The dog knew as surely as Trudie did that Knox wouldn't call.

She turned and walked away, the sun setting behind her, as she headed into the shadows. Technically, she was fine. No one actually died of a broken heart…even if they felt as if they might.

1

One and a half years later...

KNOX SETTLED Elsa's designer suitcase at the foot of the bed
in the Good Riddance Bed and Breakfast. For all the times
he'd been to Good Riddance over the years, he'd never been
inside the bed and breakfast situated on the second floor of
the air strip center. It, like the rest of the town, offered a feeling of welcome and the sense of a place out of time.

Four, maybe five guest rooms shared a communal bathroom at the end of the hall. The walls and floor were all wood.
Lace-trimmed flannel curtains hung at the window, a braided
rug covered a portion of the floor and a handmade quilt decorated the white iron bed. An old-fashioned washbasin and
water pitcher sat atop an antique stand with an oval mirror.
A small artificial tree stood in the corner, its multicolored
lights twinkling. Wooden ornaments hung on branches. Bull
Swenson was a champion whittler. Knox was certain it was
Bull's work. His grandmother would've loved it. It was only
in the last six months that he could think of Mormor without
feeling overwhelmed by desolation.

Outside, dark was already descending on this December
midday. Yet another thing that imparted a sense of the "olden

days" was the absence of street lights. Years ago the citizens of Good Riddance had voted against them. Despite the impending dark, Chrismoose preparations continued in full swing. The sounds of barking dogs, kids' laughter, snowmobiles, snatches of conversation and laughter drifted up. Bustle and excitement filled the air and a sense of homecoming filled Knox. Good Riddance had been something of a second home over the years, particularly at Chrismoose.

The celebration had become a regional draw for the small bush town. Years ago a hermit named Chris would ride his pet moose into town a few days before Christmas. Chris wore a Santa suit and always brought a sack of toys he'd spent the year carving and assembling for the kids in town. After Chris's death, Merrilee, the town founder and mayor, kept the tradition alive in his honor. It had become a weeklong festival of winter games and competitions, a talent showcase of local artists, and a Miss Chrismoose pageant.

Being here was definitely bittersweet. Since he was twelve years old, he and Mormor had attended Chrismoose with Trudie and her parents. It had become a long-standing tradition.

Early on, it was simply the hermit on his pet moose and the two families had spent time ice fishing and cross-country skiing. Chrismoose had always been one of the highlights of his year. Even once he was an adult, he still showed up to escort Mormor to Chrismoose—and Trudie and her parents were always there as well.

Trudie... He just couldn't think about her. He actually did a damn fine job not thinking of Trudie most of the time.

It had been nearly two years since he'd been in Good Riddance for Chrismoose. Last year he and Elsa had spent the week before Christmas skiing in Alyeska.... Well, he'd skied and Elsa had spent her time at the spa. She'd said they should start a new tradition, one a little more sophisticated and up-scale.

There had been another change in his holiday tradition. He'd never told Elsa about the custom he and Trudie had started as kids and continued until Mormor died—they exchanged gifts for the twelve days before Christmas instead of after. As kids they'd drawn each other pictures illustrating the verses of the song. As they'd grown older, it had morphed into a gift for each day. But there had been no gifts last year. And he had switched the damn radio station every time that song had come on.

It was ironic that Elsa had dubbed Chrismoose hokey and provincial. Once she'd pointed it out, he did kind of see it that way. But they were here this year so Elsa could preside as a visiting "dignitary." She had been heavily involved in the pageant scene since she was a teenager and had served as a judge for Anchorage's Miss Snow Queen; she'd been dubbed the long-standing Miss Snow Queen even though she no longer officially held the title.

Knox was only accompanying her as a favor. He'd told her they were done and she'd asked him to see her through this as her "date." He didn't think it was such a big deal for the Snow Queen to be escort-less but she'd asked him this favor as a parting gift, so they were here, ostensibly "together." And it was an opportunity for him to "run into" Trudie. He'd missed her—her sunny smile, her sense of adventure, her insight. But it had been so damn long, calling would be awkward. Running into her at Chrismoose would be inevitable.

"Thanks, you're a doll," Elsa said, bussing him on the cheek rather than really kissing him—she didn't want to smear her lipstick. She twirled around, her white-fur trimmed dress swirling around her. "How do I look?"

Her blonde hair appeared casually piled atop her head in a cascade of curls. However, Knox had been privy to all the preparations and knew just how much effort went into the end result. The casual style was a carefully constructed illusion. The white, fur-trimmed suit and matching mukluks with off-white, intricate beading did set off her luminous porcelain skin, though. "You're stunning." And she was. He was constantly struck by her beauty. Unfortunately, it only ran skin-deep. "You are the perfect Snow Queen."

She smiled, revealing her perfectly straight teeth, whitened to a gleaming sparkle. "Oh, you're so sweet."

No. Knox wasn't particularly sweet, but he had the drill down by now. And oddly enough his veterinary training had helped. Elsa was high-maintenance—kind of like dealing with a high-strung horse.

"Okay, gotta run. Duty calls."

"Have fun," he said as she sailed through the door.

Elsa took her duties as a visiting dignitary very seriously. She was booked in here at the bed and breakfast while Knox was at the cabin where he and Mormor used to stay. The Knudson brothers, sons of one of Mormor's friends, had a very basic cabin for hunting and fishing in the summer and had always made it available to Knox and his grandmother. Trudie and her folks stayed in a similar cabin about a mile away.

The place would truly be fraught with memories of Mormor and Trudie and her family coming and going. He hadn't broached Elsa about sharing the cabin with him. As a guest "celebrity" she needed to be accessible, which meant in town at the bed and breakfast. That made sense. And it was just as well. While Elsa's company would've kept his loss at bay, he wouldn't have to listen to her go on about how pedestrian the accommodations were. Hell, it was a hunting and fishing cabin.

Knox gave her a few minutes' head start and then he and Jessup made their way downstairs to the airstrip office where

Merrilee Danville Weatherspoon Swenson sat at her desk. She'd been elsewhere when he and Elsa had arrived and Tessa Sisnuket had shown them to Elsa's room.

"Knox Whitaker! Jessup! It's so good to see you both." She enveloped Knox in a hug and then ran her hand affectionately over Jessup's head. The dog's tail thumped against the ground.

"Hi, Merrilee. It's good to see you again, as well."

As a young teen, he'd sort of had a crush on Merrilee for a season. Even though she had to be hitting her late fifties or early sixties, she was still a pretty woman with sparkling blue eyes, a ready smile and a generous warmth that nonetheless cut straight to the chase.

He'd considered her the coolest of the cool. Damn, the woman had founded the town of Good Riddance nearly thirty years ago and turned it into the charming haven it was today. The town greeting, compliments of Merrilee, was "Welcome to Good Riddance, where you get to leave behind what ails you."

Knox had been ailing and out of sorts for so long it had simply become his state of being. He doubted that even Good Riddance could cure what ailed him since he wasn't sure what was wrong. How did you accurately treat something undiagnosed?

"I'm sorry about your Grandmother. She was a fine person."

"One of the best." It had been nearly two years and some days he still forgot she was gone.

"Well, I'm glad you're joining us again. We missed you last year, although I understand it would've probably been too painful to be here."

Knox just offered a quick, hard nod.

"Coffee?" she said. "Straight-up, right?"

"You remember."

"Of course. I'm not totally senile yet." She laughed and

he laughed along with her. She wasn't remotely senile. "Here you go."

He took the proffered cup. "Thanks."

"So, how's Trudie?"

Now that was the sixty-four-thousand-dollar question, wasn't it?

"I...uh...I haven't talked to Trudie lately." He'd never called her. Everything inside him knotted at just saying her name aloud.

They hadn't spoken, emailed, Facebooked, or Tweeted since that evening she'd walked as the summer sun sank behind the distant mountains. She'd accused him of becoming a stranger, but she was the one who'd changed. She'd been critical of him, critical of Elsa, and hadn't seemed to understand when she, as his best friend, should have understood.

He'd felt so numb, so anchorless when Mormor had died.... And Elsa had been there to fill the void. She'd seemed to wrap herself around his numbness.

Trudie had had a problem with Elsa, had seemed totally oblivious to the need Elsa filled. Elsa wouldn't have wanted him calling Trudie, but Trudie knew where to find him and she hadn't bothered. Neither had he. It had just been easier that way.

"Hmm," Merrilee said, her look full of speculation.

Knox shrugged off the question in her eyes. "Things change." He glanced around. "There are more pictures on the wall than the last time I was here." The log wall held an assortment of photos that relayed the history of Good Riddance and its inhabitants. "It still smells the same in here and welcomes the same—" the life-size moose replica in a Santa hat next to the decorated tree had been a staple for years "—but there are changes." He nodded toward the two men sitting opposite one another at a chess table. He didn't have to say it. One of the old codgers who'd been a permanent fixture there had passed just as Mormor had. A grey-haired man who was something of a sophisticated dresser, especially for Good Riddance, had taken the spot.

"True enough, things change. I expected... Well, you and Trudie were always so close." She shook her head as if clearing it. "Regardless, it's nice to see you again. We're glad you're here. How's the animal-doctoring business?"

"I can't complain. I just took on a partner." He'd known when he joined Mack Beasley's vet practice a couple of years ago that Mack was planning to retire soon. He'd done so a year and a half ago and Knox had been so swamped with work he could barely breathe. He'd have been hard-pressed to attend Chrismoose if Luke Farmington hadn't come on-board a couple of months ago. Relief vets were one thing but the real relief was having Luke to share the practice. "He's a nice guy who moved to Anchorage from Denver."

"That's wonderful. You should've brought him to Chris-moose."

The Twelve Days of Christmas started playing on the boombox over on the table. Damn—his and Trudie's song. He could hardly change it.

Knox forced a grin and tried to focus on the conversation at hand. "Someone had to stay behind to take care of the business. It looks as if things are going well here. I noticed some new buildings when we were coming in."

Merrilee nodded and was on the verge of saying one thing when something caught her eye. Like an internal alarm shrilling, the hair on the back of Knox's neck stood at attention.

"Well," Merrilee said, "you and Trudie are about to have the opportunity to catch up. She just walked through the door."

He'd known it before she said it. He'd felt Trudie's presence the way he always had. He could also feel her animosity. She was still pissed.

Damn, he might as well go ahead and get this over with. He turned.

He felt as if he'd been kicked in the stomach. It was as if he was seeing her for the first time. She was familiar, but had he ever really looked at her?

The curve of her cheek, the sensual line of her lips, the hug of her jeans to her hips. And her hair was different.

Trudie Brown was a beautiful woman.

SHE'D HEARD he would be here since Elsa was coming in her capacity as Snow Queen. She'd known she'd see him. She'd thought she was prepared. She'd thought she was over him.

She wasn't.

Knox. She stood immobilized. And that song… Seeing him was like ripping open an old wound. All the missing, wanting, hurting, surged through her anew. Yet she couldn't stop looking at him, soaking up the sight of him. She'd cried and ranted and tried so hard to forget him. She had kept herself busy, throwing herself into work, joining friends for outings, dating. But busy hadn't remedied the sleepless nights when she'd longed for him, ached for the sound of his voice, the magic of his smile.

So many times she'd thought about calling him and telling him she loved him. But their friendship hadn't meant enough for him to salvage. Why would he possibly want to know she loved him like a woman loved a man? So, she'd kept that part to herself, not even sharing it with her girlfriends.

Now here he was in front of her, all sturdy six feet of him. His dark hair was a little longer. He was perhaps a bit thinner. There were a few lines bracketing his eyes that hadn't been there before. He looked weary…but wonderful.

Thunk. Instinctively she reached back and braced her hand against the wall, barely staying upright. Jessup, all eightysomething pounds of him, was on her, licking her neck. Obviously his joy at seeing her outweighed his obedience training.

She'd missed Jessup almost as much as she'd missed Knox.

"Jessup, down!" Knox commanded in his most censuring tone. The dog glanced back at his master, but just couldn't contain his joy at seeing Trudie. She buried her face in the fur of his neck. "Hey, sweet boy. How've you been?"

Jessup licked her hand and her neck again as if to say he'd been okay but he was much better now that she was here.

Trudie straightened and dredged up a smile as she walked forward, Jessup glued to her side. "Merrilee," she said by way of greeting as Merrilee enveloped her in a hug.

"It's so good to see you again, Trudie. How are you?"

"Fine, thanks. And you?" God, she felt so awkward with Knox in the background. Funny how their lives had been so intertwined—they'd shared some of the same friends, liked to eat at the same restaurants—but they'd still managed to avoid one another for the last year and a half. Trudie found it richly ironic that she and Knox were crossing paths in a place where the town slogan was Welcome to Good Riddance, where you got to leave behind what ailed you. Apparently, she was an exception because she was coming face-to-face with what ailed her, or had ailed him.

"No complaints," Merrilee said by way of answering Trudie's inquiry.

"That's good." Okay, just say it. Do it. She finally spoke directly to him. She tried not to stare. She'd missed him so much it was hard not to soak him up like a dry sponge. "Hi, Knox."

"Hey, Trudie."

She wasn't sure what to do and neither was he. They both stepped forward, reaching for one another. Should she hug him? Shake his hand? Neither seemed right. She stepped back to where she'd started and Knox mirrored her. It all felt incredibly awkward but also rather wonderful to see him again. It felt as if it had been forever.

"It's been a while," she said. She hadn't intended to sound accusatory, but the censorious note crept in nonetheless. And Jessup was still by her side.

Merrilee looked from Trudie to Knox and nodded. "Excuse me, I need to check on something and I'm sure you two are eager to catch up."

Merrilee had neatly backed them into a corner. Either of them could hardly declare they had no interest in sitting down with the other.

"So, how have you been, Trudie?" Knox said. "You look good. Real good."

A shiver slid through her at the tone of his voice, at the words. How many times, in the last year and a half, had she wondered what it would be like if he saw her as a woman? Now it seemed that perhaps he did. "Thanks. I cut my hair."

She'd always kept her light brown hair long. Now it swung against her shoulders and bangs feathered her forehead. The hairdresser had woven in low lights and the style framed her face.

"I like it." The look in his eyes sent heat coursing through her.

Trudie nodded. "So do I." She wasn't quite sure what to do with herself and she was suddenly burning up. She unwound the scarf from her neck and tugged it off. It didn't do much to cool her down. "You look good, too."

"Thanks," he said. He shoved his hands in his blue-jean pockets and shifted from one foot to another. "Want to grab a bite to eat next door?"

She hesitated. She should say she had other things to do. She should politely decline because he was here with Elsa. She should just let him...it...them go...but Trudie found she couldn't. How much harm could come from a half-hour lunch?

She thought she'd steeled herself for seeing him again, but she wasn't immune to him. She wasn't so much hungry for food as she was to know how he was and what had been going on in his life. Half an hour, an hour tops. "Sure. You know I can always eat." She tacked on the last bit so that he didn't think sitting down at Gus's, the restaurant right next door to the bed and breakfast and the airstrip center, was personal.

Of course, Gus's was the gathering place and news spread in Good Riddance like wildfire during a drought. Elsa would know Trudie and Knox were eating together before they finished the meal. She almost asked him if that was going to be a problem but decided to keep her mouth shut.

Knox knew how things were in Good Riddance. But he was a big boy, and if his sharing a table with Trudie posed a problem with Elsa, then that was between the two of them, wasn't it?

Knox had ceased being her business when he walked out of her life.

2

Knox instructed Jessup to wait for them in the airstrip center—the dog was normally very well disciplined, but Knox cut the canine some slack. He understood. Knox had never been much of a hugger, but he'd had an almost overwhelming urge to touch Trudie, to feel her warmth next to his, to inhale her scent. He had, however, not done any of those things. He wasn't sure that Trudie would welcome a hug from him these days. He wasn't so great at people interactions but he was tuned into animals and she'd reminded him of a wounded cat that called for a very cautious approach.

He held the door leading from the airstrip to Gus's for Trudie. Her scent, the sound of her voice, her presence stirred a slew of memories—of Christmases past, nearly a lifetime past, decorating Christmas trees, cross-country skiing. She'd assisted him as he doctored a hurt cat who turned out to be Mr. Finch's feline from down the street, which had started a precedent of wounded animals seeming to find their way to him. Trudie had always been by his side to help out. He'd wondered more than once if wounded animals found their way to him when he was a kid because they'd sensed a kindred spirit in him. He'd had a connection with animals that he simply hadn't found with humans...except for Mormor and, in retrospect, Trudie.

Elsa would probably flip a bitch when she found out that he and Trudie were hanging out at Gus's, but she'd get over it. He and Trudie were just two old friends catching up and he and Elsa were only here together for appearance sake—the sake of her appearance as Snow Queen.

Gus's was jam-packed. The place was a mix of laughter and loud conversation. A soap opera blared on one of the wall-mounted televisions while "Grandma Got Run Over By a Reindeer" played at a high volume on the jukebox in the back corner. The smell of grilled food set his stomach growling.

"Wow, it's busy," Trudie said, stopping right inside the door, mainly because there wasn't enough room to continue walking.

Knox, caught unawares, bumped into the back of her. Instinctively, he grabbed her to keep from pitching forward. Instead, the back of her pressed hard against the front of him. Her hair brushed against his chin and cheek while her scent, light and innocent yet seductive, teased him. Something wild and hot coursed through him—desire of such a magnitude that he didn't initially recognize it as such. He wanted to wrap his arms around her from behind, press more firmly into the cushion of her backside, test the area of her exposed neck with his lips to see if it was as sweet as it was tantalizing.

Instead, he immediately released her. She took a half step forward as he half stepped back.

Crap, he was turned on...by Trudie. That was the feeling he'd felt when he'd first seen her, but it had been so foreign in conjunction with Trudie that he hadn't recognized it. He knew it now. Blood had rushed hard, fast and hot to his head, the one between his thighs that tended to fog the thinking of the one on his shoulders.

Trudie glanced behind at him. "Are you okay? Did I step on your toes?"

No, you rocked against my penis and turned my world upside down. "I'm fine. You didn't catch my toes. How about you? You okay?"

"Yes," she said, "but I think we're out of luck. There's no room to sit and standing room is crowded over at the bar."

Knox glanced around the room. Booths lined the wall to the right of the main doorway. Every seat at the bar was taken. More booths formed a short L shape against the back wall while tables filled the open floor space ahead of them. Both pool tables were in use and a couple of guys were arguing good-naturedly over a dart game. It didn't look as if anyone was on the verge of giving up a spot.

"You're right."

"I usually am."

He wondered how long she'd been waiting to say that. Maybe a year and a half? "We could get it to go," Knox said.

"And eat where?"

"Elsa's staying here, but I'm staying out at the cabin."

"You're at the cabin?"

"Well, I will be. I haven't made it that far yet."

"Have you been since…"

She didn't have to say it. She was asking if he'd been there since he'd lost Mormor. "No. This is the first time." He paused and she said it before he could ask.

"Do you want me there?"

He hadn't realized it until that instant, but he didn't hesitate. "Yes."

She paused. "What about Elsa?"

He deliberately answered as if he'd misunderstood. "She's busy with some Chrismoose activities. I think she had an interview over at the community center with a newspaper person. You want a burger?" Trudie loved burgers, fries and a good, cold beer.

"Sure. Medium—"

"Well," he finished. He knew what she liked, at least food-wise. Now he was foolishly burning to know what she liked in other respects. Did she like kissing? How did she like to be kissed? How had he missed the tempting, succulent full-ness of her lower lip? Was her neck sensitive? How did she like to be touched? And that was some dangerous thought paths to follow.... He brought his attention back to burgers and beers. "And I have some Mad Moose in the ice chest."

They'd "discovered" the micro-brewed beer about eight years ago.

"But of course," Trudie said with a smile that struck him as a bit forced. He knew the feeling.

"Wait here and I'll go put in our order."

The wait was saved from awkwardness when several peo-ple stopped by to chat, many to offer condolences for his grandmother. Surprisingly, given how crowded the place was, a quarter of an hour later they were making their way out of Gus's, to-go boxes in hand.

They stopped by the airstrip and picked up Jessup. A sense of déjà vu washed over him. It was so much like old times—her, him, the dog. Yet it was all different and had changed so drastically. Showed how deceptive outward appearances could be.

"How are your parents? Are they here?" Knox said as they stepped out onto the sidewalk. Snow crunched under-foot. Christmas lights winked and blinked in the business windows lining the street. Snow drifted down lazily while children played with a puppy on the corner, their laughter mingling with the pup's shrill bark.

"They're both fine, just really busy. Mom's got meetings she can't get out of until later in the week and you know Dad isn't going anywhere without her so they'll be up in a couple of days."

Trudie's folks had gotten married in high school when Harriet had turned up pregnant. They were one of those rare cases where things had worked out and they'd not only stayed together but were incredibly devoted to one another. They each had their own interests, but Eldon Brown would never come to Chrismoose without Harriet.

Knox nodded. "You're actually here a little earlier than usual," he said as he steered her.

"I came ahead to get the cabin set up and to help with the floral stuff." Trudie had always loved flowers and had an artistic streak to boot so it had been a no-brainer when she'd gone to work with a floral center and had done quite well at it. Knox knew she ultimately wanted to have her own shop one day…or at least that had been the plan once upon a time.

She paused as if unsure whether to continue and then obviously chose to go ahead. "They've missed you. Mom worries about you."

Something inside him turned over, touched by her words. Funny how much it meant to hear that Harriet Brown worried about him. He'd been an orphan at the age of eight, but with Mormor he'd never felt like one. He didn't suppose that twenty-eight year old men could feel orphaned, but dammit, he had when he lost Mormor. It had been traumatic when his parents had died, but Mormor had anchored him and he'd adjusted.

None of that had been the case when he lost Mormor. In retrospect, he realized he'd been in a state of shock when he'd hooked up with Elsa. In a normal world and with rightful thinking, Trudie and her parents would've been a comfort. But there was nothing normal or right about losing Mormor, and in a crazy way the Browns were part of what he'd lost so he'd distanced himself. But now…with time and more time…it was damn nice to hear that Harriet Brown had worried about him...that they still cared about him. Elsa and her folks were nice, but it simply wasn't the same. He realized at that moment just how much he'd missed the Browns. And Trudie.

"That's good to hear." He opened the truck door for her and Jessup jumped in ahead of her. Trudie followed the dog into the cab. "I've stayed away too long," Knox said.

She busied herself clicking her seatbelt into place. "Yes, you have," she said without looking at him.

He closed her door, rounded the cab, and climbed in on the other side. Jessup, the big sap, had his head on Trudie's thigh and was gazing up at her adoringly. Knox, rather confusingly, was feeling the same ever since she'd backed into him and awoken an awareness of her as a woman.

All these years, she'd been his buddy who happened to be a girl. Now, it was as if scales had suddenly dropped from his eyes and he saw her for the beautiful, sexy woman she was.

"Nice truck," she said, interrupting his thought, which was just as well.

"Thanks. I got it last year." Elsa had told him he needed something newer, bigger, faster—something that reflected who he really was. He liked it well enough, but he was just getting it to the point that it was broken in and comfortable.

He glanced over at Trudie, her profile etched in dark relief, familiar yet unfamiliar. He tightened his fingers around the steering wheel to keep from reaching over and tracing the curve of her cheek, wrapping his hand around the nape of her neck and tugging her to meet him until he felt her lips against his and tasted her mouth.

How many times had they shared the cab of his truck? Innumerable, but this time was different. Was it the truck? Was it her? Him? All of the above? Hell if he knew, he just knew it was.

He'd never been turned on by Trudie before. Apparently he was making up for lost time.

TRUDIE WAS surprised she could still actually breathe. Sharing the confines of the cab with Knox was simultaneously torturous and wonderful. Outside it was dark, cold and snowy. In here it simply smelled like man and dog…and unfortunately, Elsa's perfume. Regardless, Trudie had more than missed Knox. She'd ached for him, been bereft without him. She would not, however, fall back into that feeling, that trap.

Outside, light spilled out of the storefronts lining Main Street, the windows decorated for the season—some more native-inclined, some geared toward the religious celebration, while others were simply festooned with ribbons, lights and greenery. A makeshift RV city had been set up in the empty lot that was the baseball diamond in the summer. A few hardy souls had actually pitched tents, but for the most part it was travel-trailers behind trucks and motor homes. Trudie noticed a psychedelic painted school bus with a big peace sign on the front hood. The Hatchers were here. They'd been coming for years. It really wouldn't be Chrismoose without them, just as it hadn't really been Chrismoose last season without Knox and Mormor. She had missed him.

"So, have you missed me?" Knox said.

His question startled her. She and Knox had spent so much time together for so long they used to complete one another's sentences, but she'd figured some of that connection would have been lost. She certainly didn't want him tapping into all of her thoughts and feelings. However, it had always been part relief and part frustration that he'd never tapped into the way she really felt about him. Now would be a bad time to start. Still, after the chasm that had separated them for the past couple of years, it was a little uncanny that his question echoed her thought.

"Have you missed me?" she countered. She tensed inside. His answer meant far more to her than it should have at this juncture. She needed to keep her perspective.

She caught the flash of white teeth as he grinned in the glow of the dashboard, the storefront lights of Good Riddance having been left behind. His smile set off her pulse like a runaway train. The headlights illuminated the world of snowy white around them. "I asked you first," he said.

Trudie swallowed her disappointment at his nonanswer. She needed to lighten up. "Of course I have. I haven't found anyone else I can beat at Scrabble as mercilessly as I can beat you."

He laughed, the warm, rich sound filling the cabin, washing over her like warm water. "Ha."

"You asked."

"I did, didn't I?"

Jessup settled his head more firmly on her thigh and she absently rubbed his soft fur with her left hand, finding comfort in the familiar contours and the press of his weight against her leg.

There was an arousing familiarity to Knox's hands on the steering wheel—broad, strong hands. Heaven knew how much in the last year and a half she'd longed to feel his hands, his mouth, his skin against hers in the throes of passion. She had thought she'd finally put that behind her.

But, she couldn't leave the issue Knox had raised alone. She'd answered his inquiry, now he could do the same. "You've missed me?"

"Sure. No one makes chocolate chip cookies quite like you do." There was a forced heartiness to his declaration.

She'd set the standard with the Scrabble statement but nonetheless she wanted to bang him over the head. Her cookies? He'd missed her damn cookies?

He sighed quietly in the silence. "I have missed you,

Trudie." He paused, the words hanging between them, weaving deep into her soul, cracking through the hard shell she'd encased her heart in. "I'm sorry I never called."

Suddenly everything seemed much better in her world with that one simple admission and his apology. "Thanks."

While it was good to hear, where did it leave them? Pretty much nowhere. She consciously dialed herself back. She'd never trusted anyone the way she'd trusted Knox and he'd turned his back on her. He'd flat out walked away and left her standing alone and hurting and she'd be damned if she was willing to go there with him again. She'd be all kinds of a fool to open herself to that…and she was a lot of things but she wasn't a fool.

"We were good friends—" she knew he wouldn't miss the past tense there "—so of course we've missed one another, but that's kind of life, isn't it? There's an ebb and flow to everything, especially relationships. We ebbed. It happens." She shrugged. Once again, she reminded herself to lighten things up. "So, did you do any fishing last season? I caught a forty-pound halibut last year."

Knox whistled beneath his breath, impressed. She hadn't set a record or anything, but as fishing went it was big. "Homer?"

She and Knox had made the trip numerous times since they were teenagers. Homer, down on the Kenai Peninsula, offered the best halibut fishing in Alaska. "Of course. You caught anything good lately?"

"I haven't been in a couple of years."

"What?" Okay, she knew it was Elsa but she was going to play it. What the heck? Knox loved to fish. "You haven't been fishing?"

"I've been busy."

Busy? If she needed any confirmation—which she didn't—that Elsa was so totally wrong for him, there it was. Of course, she could know it all day, but until he figured it out... "That's a shame. Life's too busy when you can't take at least one day off or an afternoon."

"Yeah. I know. But I'm going this spring."

"Well, that's good. You've got to make time for the things you love." She found it sad, but in a way oddly comforting, that Knox hadn't been fishing. She'd thought he must not care about her if she hadn't heard from him, but if he hadn't even been fishing, and she knew how he felt about fishing...

"I know," he said, acknowledging her assertion that it was necessary to make time for cherished things. "So, who'd you go fishing with?"

He'd asked her countless times in the past what she'd done and who she'd done it with, but this time his question held a studied casualness. He was quizzing her.

"Dad and I went a couple of times and then I went with a friend."

"Anyone I know?" There was nothing casual about the question.

"I don't think so. Jeremy Lyons."

"No. I don't know him." His tone was clipped. "Where'd you meet him?"

"At the fishing supply store. We were both checking out the lures." She'd immediately liked the stocky, compact guy with the ginger hair.

"Ah. I see. So, have you seen him outside of fishing?"

Technically, it was none of Knox's business, but she had nothing to hide. "We've been out to dinner a couple of times, caught a few movies." They genuinely had a good time together...except he wasn't Knox, which was irrationally confounding.

"Is he coming to Chrismoose?"

Once again, she was really close to telling him it was none of his business. There was a time when they would give one another the thumbs-up or thumbs-down on who the other one was dating. That, however, had all changed with Elsa. "Not that I'm aware of." Jeremy had asked to come. She had told him she'd be busy and accommodations were sparse. She hadn't offered him to stay at the cabin with her.

"You like him?"

"He's a nice enough guy or I wouldn't hang out with him, would I?" Actually, she had stopped seeing so much of Jeremy because he was obviously feeling for her what, at this point, she couldn't feel for him.

"Guess not."

The crunch of tires over the packed snow was the only sound in the truck. Coming with Knox had been a mistake. At the least she should've driven her vehicle rather than leaving it in the parking lot in town. Instead of the comfortable silences they'd once enjoyed, this was awkward.

She was altogether too aware of him and her longing for him intensified. Longing was too weak a word. Perhaps it was all the nights of fantasizing about him, dreaming of his touch, his hands on her, her hands on him, heated kisses in the dark, the feel of him thrusting between her thighs. Moisture had gathered there when she was simply sharing the cab with him and she felt as if she might explode from the throbbing ache.

Trying to distract herself, Trudie stared out the window, absently noting the enormous evergreens, their branches hanging heavy with snow. They simply looked sad to her.

Knox tapped his finger against the steering wheel and then reached over and turned on the CD player. The sound of Johnny Cash and June Carter Cash filled the air. At least Knox was staying true to the music he liked. Elsa must approve. Trudie knew it was a catty thought. It'd be one thing if she thought Knox was happy, but he wasn't. Trudie had seen it in his eyes.

Once again she thought she'd made a mistake coming with

him when she was fairly humming with want, but she was committed. They'd have their burgers and beer and he could take her back to get her SUV and that would be that.

She wasn't quite sure why the thought didn't cheer her up.

3

KNOX PULLED UP to the front of the cabin and killed the engine. They let the silence and dark adjust around them.

"Hang tight," he said, opening his door and stepping out into the freshly shoveled area, the snow beneath his boots hard and compact. He rounded the truck and opened the passenger door for Trudie.

She slid out of the cab. Jessup reluctantly followed. It was a helluva note that a dog born and raised in Alaska didn't like the snow. All the malamutes and huskies wanted to romp in the snow—Jessup just wanted to get the hell out of the stuff.

"I see Petey's been here," Trudie said.

Knox handed Trudie the take-out boxes. "I knew it'd be dark by the time I got Elsa settled and then got out here." He grabbed the soft-sided cooler out of the back seat. "And you know how much I like shoveling snow." For twenty bucks Petey, the part-time prospector who also ran the closest thing to a taxi service in Good Riddance, had come out and cleared a path to the front door. It had been worth every cent.

Trudie laughed. "Yeah, it's not high on my top-ten list of ways to spend my time."

Knox unlocked the door and reached inside, flipping on the light switch. Jessup pushed past them—he was a good dog even if he was a wimp. Knox motioned for Trudie to precede him. Her arm brushed against him and heat flashed through him. He entered behind her, closing the door, leaving the dark and snow on the other side.

He simply stood still for a moment as memories and Mormor's absence washed over him. He'd thought he was ready for this, but he wasn't so sure now. He was glad Trudie was here.

Ironically, while everything in his life and his world had changed, nothing had changed inside the cabin.

It remained one big room with a small half-bath off to the side. A pullout sofa and armchair upholstered in a worn plaid dominated one half of the room. The kitchen, with a scarred oak table and mismatched chairs, sat on the other. A loft ran across the back of the cabin, a ladder granting access. Up top was a double bed where Knox had always bunked down. Below, tucked beneath the loft area, was another double bed that had been Mormor's sleep spot. A pot-bellied wood-burning stove sat between the sofa and the bathroom. A Big Mouth Billy Bass singing fish was mounted on the wall over the sofa. The Knudson brothers had always had a sense of humor.

Memories of laughter and Chrismooses past crowded him. He sprang into action, which struck him as a far better plan than drowning in nostalgia.

"I'll get the stove started." It was so cold inside the cabin, their breath formed smoke rings. "It'll warm up in no time."

Petey had also laid a fire in the stove. Knox just needed to light it. Within minutes warmth began to dissipate the room's chill.

He sat on the sagging plaid sofa and Trudie perched in the matching chair. So much for her sharing the sofa with him but it was just as well because Trudie had become temptation incarnate. He laughed as he eyed the take-out containers on the scarred coffee table. "Now that the burgers and fries are cold…"

Trudie laughed in return. "Hey, they go with the beer."

"Remember when—"

"Remember when—"

They spoke simultaneously.

"You ran out of gas?" Trudie said. They'd planned to go fishing and picked up some burgers, figuring they could make the trip there and back without gassing up. They'd been wrong.

Knox nodded. "Yep. The burgers were cold in the cab…"

"And the beer froze back in the truck bed."

"I know," Knox said. "That's when I started using a cooler and putting it behind the seat."

For a few seconds their awkwardness disappeared in the shared memory. Knox bit into the burger. As always it was cooked to perfection. One of Lucky's signature touches was topping each burger with grilled onions—grilled but still crunchy. "Even cold Lucky's burgers are good."

"I know," Trudie said, speaking around a mouthful.

The firewood popped and snapped merrily in the stove and a contentment he'd not known for a long time stole through him. An awareness he'd never had before was present—an awareness of Trudie as not just a buddy but a woman. The lamp on the end table between the chair and couch etched her features against the shadows beyond.

Her straight nose had the slightest tilt at the end and her chin came to a cute point. Her hair curved slightly toward her cheeks and he noticed how her cheekbones defined her face. She was beautiful in a way he'd never noticed before— not the in-your-face coiffed beauty of Elsa, but warmer, less manufactured. Elsa was like a flawlessly groomed Persian cat while Trudie was a short-haired Siamese.

As with any other animal, the Persian and Siamese were

both great breeds, it was just a matter of what suited your taste.

"So, I'm actually participating in Chrismoose this year," Trudie said, as if grasping for something to say. She looked slightly uncomfortable. He supposed he had been staring.

"How's that?"

"Well, it's gotten bigger and Merrilee asked me if I'd work in some floral arrangements. One of the things we discussed was keeping it true to the area. Tomorrow I'm on the hunt for materials."

"Need any help?"

Trudie paused and he could practically see the wheels turning in her head. Finally, she spoke. "Look, I want to keep things smooth and calm in my life. I don't want you coming with me if it's going to stir up tension with Elsa. That's not why I'm here and that's not what I want." She looked past him to the stove. "It took me some time to work through missing you, not having you in my life. I don't want to go through that adjustment again."

"I'm sorry—"

"You've already apologized and I've accepted. I'm not looking for another apology. I'm just saying I don't want to argue over Elsa again, I don't want Elsa giving you ultimatums and one day you're in my life and the next day you're not."

"It sounds as if you're giving ultimatums now."

Trudie shrugged. "Maybe, although I don't think so. I'm just being straight-up with you."

It was Knox's turn to pause. He wanted to tell Trudie the deal—that he was only here with Elsa for appearance's sake, that he and Elsa were on the exit plan—but that didn't quite seem right. He also wanted to tell her that Elsa wouldn't make it an issue, but she would. He was beginning to see things a little more clearly than he had in a long time.

However he could handle Elsa. As for Trudie's other concern— "So, I'm not doing another disappearing act again. What time do you want to get started tomorrow?"

TRUDIE DIDN'T KNOW how she felt. If someone were to peer through the window, things would look the same as they had for years—she and Knox chatting and sharing a meal. Yet, everything was different. Who was he? Who was she? What did she want?

"Did you bring the tree?" she asked.

It was an artificial tree. As children, she and Knox had made salt dough ornaments for it. They'd sat at Mormor's kitchen table and cut shapes with cookie cutters and afterwards painted them with craft paint. Every year, when they came to Chrismoose, they set up the tree on the first night of their arrival so they could enjoy it the entire time they were in Good Riddance.

Knox offered a quick nod. "It's in the truck."

She inwardly heaved a sigh of relief. If he had let the tree and those ornaments go in the estate sale or donated them to a charity, she would've lost it with him. "I could help you set it up…or would you rather do it when I'm not here?"

"Let's do it together," he said.

She knew what he meant but she couldn't seem to stop her mind from spinning the image to the two of them doing it together. The taste of his kisses, the stroke of his tongue, the heat of his hands against her skin, teasing, caressing, exploring… Heat rose in her face and she hoped Knox was oblivious to her reaction. Rather than look at him, she focused her attention on Jessup stretched out by the stove. "Do you need some help getting it in?" Whoa…wait…that sounded so wrong… "I mean from the truck to the cabin, or do you want me to babysit Jessup?"

"You keep warm with Muttzilla. I'll get it."

Knox pushed to his feet and shrugged back into his jacket. Frigid air blasted the cabin when he opened the door. Within minutes he was back, wrestling the oblong box and a smaller rectangular one through the door then closing it with his booted foot.

Trudie laughed and Knox grimaced. "Glad I can amuse you."

"Me too," she shot back, laughing harder, and then he was laughing, too, and she wasn't even sure what was so funny but it was and that was the way it used to be—one of them would get tickled and then the other one would start laughing and neither of them could particularly remember why.

Now their laughter trailed off and awareness blossomed between them. Trudie's breath caught in her throat and her heartbeat quickened as she lost herself in the depths of his eyes, in the shared moment, in simply being with him again.

Jessup nudged her knee with his nose and she looked away from Knox. "So…Jessup's ready to put up the tree." Her voice came out husky.

"Well, we want Jessup to be happy so let's get to it." Knox laughed, pulled out his pocketknife and cut through the tape that held the tree box together.

It wasn't until she hit her early twenties that the irony of Mormor's Christmas tree hit Trudie. They lived in a land of evergreens, yet Mormor's tree of choice was artificial white tinsel.

"Want to make some hot chocolate while I get the lights on?" Knox said. It was traditionally what they did. Mormor and Trudie would make hot cocoa while Knox set the tree up and strung the lights.

"Sure. I can do that."

Trudie rummaged around in the kitchen, which was hauntingly familiar even though she hadn't set foot inside it for nearly two years. While the water boiled she pulled out the envelopes of cocoa mix and dumped them in mugs. The steaming cups were ready just as he finished assembling the tree and stringing the lights, which was pretty much the way they'd always done it.

Trudie passed Knox his drink. His fingers brushed against hers in the exchange and a shiver coursed through her, derailing her. She'd never shivered like that when Jeremy Lyons's fingers merely glanced against hers. Heck, they'd shared a kiss or two that hadn't left her with even a quiver…unfortunately.

Lucky her. It had to be Knox, here with his Ms. Snow Queen girlfriend. Knox who had walked away from their friendship and subsequently broken her heart. Wasn't that just grand and then some?

"Delicious," he said after a cautious sip. It was hot. "Thanks."

"You're welcome," she said. It was impossible for her to stay angry with him. He was simply too dear to her and she'd missed him too much and she didn't know when they'd have time like this together again. She refused to squander it.

Trudie tweaked a couple of the white tinsel branches, positioning them more advantageously. "Okay. Ready for the decorations?"

Jessup sat with his head resting on his paws, watching, as they hung the ornaments they'd fashioned as children.

While the whole process could have had a melancholy feel about it, it was simply nice. Rather than being sad because Mormor wasn't here, Trudie found the memories comforting.

Then they did what they'd always done. They turned out all of the lights except for the ones on the tree and settled next to each other on the couch.

There was something mesmerizing, relaxing, about the twinkling lights, the taste of hot cocoa, the scent and crackle of wood burning, and most of all the solidness and warmth of

Knox next to her. Her eyes and body grew heavier. She lowered her guard enough to settle against his side. The steadiness of his heartbeat was beneath her shoulder, his breath stirred against the edge of her hair. She rested her head in the crook of his shoulder. He smelled faintly of antiseptic and leather and wood smoke.

She should get up and leave. She should have him take her back to town to pick up her vehicle or at least to her own cabin down the way. She would. She'd insist...in a few minutes. She just wanted a little more time with him, like this. She wanted to close her eyes and pretend...for just a bit longer...that he was hers.

"Trudie?"

"Um?"

"This is nice."

He wrapped his arm around her and something inside her melted. It was as if her heart had been frozen since that night they'd parted ways at sunset. She snuggled deeper into his embrace. His muscles bunched against her side. His scent, familiar and particular to him, crept around her.

The fire crackled in the stove and the tattoo of his heart beat against her ear. In the far distance the hum of snowmobiles paired with the high-pitched barking of a team of sled dogs.

A delicious, languid heat stole through her. She felt like a tightly closed bud unfurling in warmth and light.

His arm tightened around her and she glanced at him in inquiry. Everything shifted between them though neither actually moved. His breath, warm and fragrant with chocolate, teased against her hair and her temple.

He leaned down slightly and she angled her face, her lips parting slightly, hungry, eager for his kiss. Confusion, desire warred within his blue eyes. She saw it, felt it—he wanted her. His lips were a fraction of an inch from hers when the thought of Elsa inserted itself between them.

No! She couldn't do this. She shifted her mouth out of range of his. "It's time for me to leave."

4

WELL, THAT HAD damn near been a very stupid move on his part. Knox sat up straight, removing his arm from her shoulder. Undoubtedly, undisputedly, kissing Trudie would've been a mistake. Wouldn't it?

She stood, hesitating. "I need to use your bathroom before we leave."

"Sure. No problem."

She crossed the floor, closing the door behind her.

Of course, it would've been a mistake. He'd thought the sexual tension, the awareness, had been shared. Uh, apparently not. He'd only almost kissed her and she'd reacted like a scalded cat.

He pulled on his jacket and readied hers. He suddenly couldn't wait to get her out of here—to get away from her. She was screwing with his comfort level. She left him squirming, feeling uncertain, unsettled. So, yeah, she was right—it was time for her to go.

The toilet flushed and a few minutes later she exited the bathroom. "Here ya go," he said, holding up her jacket.

He had planned to hold it for her while she put it on. She took it from him instead and shrugged into it herself. That was fine. Message received.

"Ready?" he said.

"Sure."

Jessup, tuned in to what was going on around him, trotted over to the front door and stood waiting. Knox opened the door and cold air rushed in. The three of them stepped out into the late-afternoon dark. "Your cabin?" he asked.

The cabin Trudie and her folks stayed in was maybe a half mile as the crow flew and about a mile by road.

"I need to pick up my car and it's in Good Riddance," she said, as she opened the truck door and waited on Jessup to hop in ahead of her.

Knox started the trip back to Good Riddance. Silence, uncomfortable and awkward, stretched between them. He glanced over at Trudie. She was staring out the window.

He should've just kissed her. How much more awkward could it be than this? And at least he'd have satisfied the need to taste her, to sample the plush fullness of her lower lip. What was the worst thing that could happen if he kissed her?

What the hell? He stopped the truck and threw it into park.

Trudie whipped her head around. "What—?"

Jessup's bulk was between them, but he grasped the nape of her neck and pulled her to him, leaning in toward her. He claimed Trudie's mouth.

Sweet…hot…heady. After a moment of hesitant surprise, her lips molded and melded to his. They were even softer than he thought they would be. Sighing into his mouth, she wound her fingers into his hair. He delved into the moist recess with his tongue, deeper, harder. Trudie leaned into him, tangling her tongue with his. A blue flame of heat flashed through him.

Trudie moaned low in the back of her throat and the sound reverberated through his mouth…and shot straight to his dick. He wanted…needed…closer.

Something butted him. Again. Jessup.

He released her. Their ragged breathing—hers and his, not the dog's—filled the cab. The windows had fogged over.

Trudie retreated to her side. Knox shifted to find a more comfortable position for his suddenly very tight pants.

"Why did you do that?" she asked.

He straightened, put the truck in gear, and resumed driving as much to forestall the temptation to kiss her again as to get to Good Riddance. "Because things were so awkward between us. And now we know."

"What is it we know other than you had no right to do that?"

"We know how good it is." It was devastatingly good.

She crossed her arms over her chest. "Don't do that again."

"Okay." It would happen again, but next time it would be her move. For as eager as he'd been to get rid of her ten minutes ago, now he didn't want her to leave. He didn't know when he would see her again and he wasn't sure exactly where she fit into his life anymore, but he didn't want her out of his life the way she had been.

"I'm heading out to the bison ranch tomorrow just for a quick visit to check out their operation and meet the resident vet. Want to tag along? It should be interesting and when we get back we could look for some of your greenery or whatever you're going to need."

Silence stretched between them. Finally she spoke. "Is Elsa coming along?"

"No. Elsa's busy with Chrismoose stuff." Plus, he hadn't asked her.

"What time are you heading out? You driving or flying?"

"Given all the snow on the roads and time constraints, I'm flying. Dalton's taking me out around nine."

Dalton Saunders and Juliette Sorenson were the bush pilots running flights out of Good Riddance. Knox would've been fine with either one. Both had gotten married since the last time he'd been here. Dalton had married the local doctor while Juliette had wound up with a construction guy. The Sisnukett cousins, Clint and Nelson, were also both hitched. Gus and Teddy had both married and left. Damn, even Merrilee and Bull had tied the knot. Elsa had started making marriage noises and that's when Knox had figured it was time for him to be making exit noises.

"You taking Jessup?" Trudie said, worrying her lower lip in consideration.

"Yep. He'd be miserable otherwise." Jessup still goes to the office with me every day." Jessup loved to be in the thick of things but he was also well-mannered so taking him along was never a problem.

"I have to work—"

"I said I'd help you, woman." He suddenly really, really wanted her to come with him. It was as if he was trying to catch up on missed time while they were both in the same place and they had the familiarity of Good Riddance and Chrismoose knitting them together. Who knew what would happen when they returned to Anchorage. He wanted to be with her while he could. Well, and there was that awesomely explosive kiss. "Come with me. Please."

He saw the capitulation in her eyes even before she nodded her head and opened her mouth. "Okay. What time? Where?"

Tomorrow was now something to anticipate. "I'll meet you at the airstrip at eight forty-five. Or I can swing by and pick you up at your place."

He pulled into the parking lot and angled his truck behind her little Suzuki SUV.

"No," she said. "I'll meet you at the airstrip."

"Okay, then." She reached for the door handle. Her vehicle was squeezed into a spot on the other side of Gus's. "Thanks for helping put up the tree."

"Right. Thanks for the burger and beer."

"No problem."

She hesitated, her hand still on the door latch. Oh boy, she had something to say and she was working herself up to spitting it out. Knox steeled himself because chances were he wasn't going to want to hear it. Trudie had never been one for mincing words.

"I know we already covered it, but I just want to make sure.... Don't kiss me again," she said, staring straight ahead, out the windshield at the snow, which had started to pepper down. Her words had a clipped edge.

She looked at him and a measure of desperation gleamed in her eyes.

"No problem." He'd always been tuned in to Trudie in a way he wasn't tuned in to anyone else. Animals and Trudie he felt most comfortable with. Trudie had wanted that kiss as much as he had…but, next time she'd kiss him. "That request would carry a little more weight if you hadn't kissed me back so enthusiastically, but okay."

"You're delusional." She tilted her little nose into the air.

"Like hell." He expected more of her. She wasn't like other women and he supposed he held her to a different standard— one that didn't cover this bullshit. "You wanted me to kiss you, but okay, we'll play this your way. You're right. You were just the innocent party sitting there all snuggled up next to me on the couch, and when you looked up at me you weren't inviting me to kiss you. And you didn't enjoy that kiss here in the truck at all. Okey dokey, if that's the way you want to remember it."

"You're not nice anymore."

"Then don't come with me tomorrow if I'm so not nice," he said, throwing out the challenge.

"I don't know you anymore."

"Then get to know me again."

She opened the door and cold rushed in, carrying a miniature snow flurry on a gust of wind.

"I'll see you tomorrow morning," she said as she climbed out.

It was a start.

TRUDIE HESITATED as Knox threw his truck in reverse and backed out of the parking lot. She'd done the right thing telling him they weren't going down that road again. Really, it was best that way…even if her body still felt like it was on fire from that one kiss. She'd known it was wrong, he was involved with Elsa, and dangerous, as evidenced by how miserable she'd been the last year and a half. However, she hadn't had the willpower to resist his touch, the feel of his lips.

Speak, or think, rather, of the devil… Elsa materialized out of nowhere.

"Hello, Gertrude."

Trudie loathed her full name, but with guilt gnawing at her over that kiss, she let it slide. "Hi, Elsa."

"It's been a long time." Elsa, resplendent in a white fur-trimmed hat and coat, tilted her head to one side. "I almost didn't recognize you with that cute haircut."

And what the heck did someone say to that? There was something faintly insulting about the term *cute* when it was wielded by a tall, elegant blonde.

"It's me." A lame response but she really didn't have anything to say to Elsa and Trudie wasn't very good at making chitchat, especially with someone she didn't like.

"How's the…what is it…oh, yes, the flower shop business?"

"No complaints. How's the fashion business?" Elsa owned a trendy boutique in Anchorage and a secondary business that catered to pageants.

"Busy, busy, busy. You should stop by some time and let

us give you a wardrobe makeover." Trudie knew Elsa meant the suggestion as a criticism, as in Trudie needed to dress more fashionably.

"Maybe I will. Sometime." Right around when hell froze over.

"Have you been to the new spa in town? It's fabulous. You should give it a try."

Elsa was brimming with what Trudie should do. And it wasn't as if Elsa had cornered the market on all things feminine. Trudie nodded. "I love Jenna's place. If you haven't had a massage from Ellie Sisnukett, you're in for a treat."

"I had a facial. You should definitely have one."

Enough. If Elsa told Trudie one more time what she should do, Trudie was probably going to scream...and screaming would be bad. She'd been civil but now she was done. "Okay, well, see you around."

Elsa either wasn't catching the hint or didn't care. She kept chatting. "So, this must be like old home week with Knoxie."

Knoxie? Elsa, a grown woman, had just referred to an adult male as Knoxie? She was letting Trudie know that she knew that Trudie and Knox had been in Gus's and left together... and she was reminding Trudie that she had been calling the shots for the last couple of years and had kept Trudie and Knox apart. There was a whole lot that was said, yet unspoken, in that one statement.

Trudie didn't like Elsa any better now than she had before and she had no intention of discussing "Knoxie" with the woman.

"Something like that," Trudie said. "Gotta run. I have a meeting in five minutes."

It was more like ten minutes but she did need to touch base with Merrilee about the floral arrangements before meeting with the new bed and breakfast owner, Alyce Henderson.

"I'm popping over to Tessa Sisnukett's screening room for a photo shoot and interview. It's some lady named Norris with the local paper and then a representative from Alaska magazine. They're doing a spread." Elsa rolled her eyes. "We had to flip-flop the schedule, which is what happens when you work with small-town affairs. Last year's Ms. Chrismoose is going to be there but I'm the big draw since I'm not local."

"Enjoy." No doubt she would…since it would be all about her.

"You, too."

Trudie skipped the pie at Gus's and entered the airstrip, relieved to be out of the cold but mostly thrilled to be away from Elsa. Dwight and Jefferson sat next to the pot-bellied stove, the chess board between them, knee-deep in a game and a lively discussion.

Merrilee, on the phone, held up her index finger in the universal give-me-a-minute-or-two gesture. Trudie nodded and stopped off at the beverage center, which usually had sweets to choose from as well. Yes. There was a plate of cookies— gingerbread—and muffins. She grabbed a cookie…and then another, and poured a cup of coffee. She pretended the gingerbread woman was Elsa and promptly bit the head off with a macabre satisfaction.

Still munching, coffee in hand, Trudie crossed the room. She didn't want Merrilee to feel rushed with her phone call and Trudie wasn't in any kind of hurry. She had plenty of time until her meeting with Alyce.

Alberta, the Gypsy Queen and Dwight's "bride"—which was pretty cute considering Dwight was an octogenarian and Alberta couldn't be far behind—sat on the love seat talking to a brunette Trudie had never met. A Christmas tree covered in moose ornaments stood between the love seat and the back door of the airstrip. The decoration that

Trudie had loved since she was a kid was the full-size moose statue decked out in a Santa costume. That moose always left her smiling.

Silk poinsettias attached to hair combs decorated Alberta's flame-red hair. She was wearing a red, green and black plaid jacket trimmed in gold tinsel down the front, the neckline and sleeves, and had paired it with full-legged gauchos in a Santa-in-his-sleigh print. Green vinyl boots—sweet mercy, Trudie had never seen a pair of green vinyl boots in her life— completed the ensemble. Alberta was colorful in every aspect of the word and then some. She motioned Trudie over as if she was directing a plane landing on a runway. Trudie knew Alberta from way back.

How the Grinch Stole Christmas played on the television in the corner. It struck Trudie as fairly appropriate considering she'd just run into Elsa in the parking lot. You had to love dark humor.

"What's shaking, sugar?" Alberta said. "How ya been?" It was obviously a rhetorical question since Alberta didn't pause to draw a breath before she continued talking. "I want you to meet someone. This is Tansy Wellington. She's a love professional, too."

Wow, wow and oh, wow. Trudie was unashamedly a fangirl. She did, however, try not to gush. "I love your column," she said. "It's a pleasure to meet you."

Trudie had thought more than once about writing to Tansy on her blog advice column when Knox and Elsa had first gotten together. She also remembered reading about an incident this past fall when a deranged woman had tried to kill Tansy. It had been a watered-down *Fatal Attraction*, Alaska-style.

The petite brunette smiled and pushed her dark-rimmed glasses more firmly onto her nose. "It's nice to meet you as well."

"Take a load off and fill us in," Alberta said, motioning toward the overstuffed armchair. Trudie sank into the thick cushion and Alberta cocked her head to one side, rather like a colorful bird. "I saw you with Knox earlier and then I saw her highness. What's up with that love triangle?"

"There's no love triangle," Trudie said.

She sipped at her coffee as Alberta's painted-on eyebrows hiked an inch up her forehead at Trudie's declaration. "If you say so."

Tansy spoke up. "Are you talking about the tall blonde woman, Miss Snow Queen, and the dark-haired man who was with her?"

"Right," Alberta said. "Those two…and of course," she indicated Trudie, "this one."

Tansy nodded. "They were checking in earlier when my flight arrived. My fiancé has a survivalist training camp up north. I fly in periodically and stay with my sister and her family," she said specifically to Trudie. "I wasn't about to miss Chrismoose. Liam and Dirk—his cousin works with him—can survive without me for the next week. No pun intended."

Trudie laughed, instantly liking the columnist.

Tansy eyed Trudie through her spectacles. "Have you ever written to me?"

"No, but I did think about it a couple of times."

Alberta chimed in. "I've seen Elsa and Knox together and she's not right for him," she said to Tansy.

"I second that," the advice columnist said. "I only saw them briefly this morning, but it was enough."

"The vote's unanimous." Alberta offered up a snort of laughter.

"It doesn't matter if the whole world knows it as long as he's still somewhere in la-la land and can't see it," Trudie said.

Alberta and Tansy exchanged a look. Tansy dipped her head toward Alberta. "Your professional take?"

"He's beginning to wake up. Men do that, you know, sort of fall under a woman's spell. It doesn't mean either one's bad, just wrong for each other." Alberta turned to Trudie. "Stay your course. He needs you."

Trudie shook her head. She wasn't going to get caught up in their love advice and matchmaking. She'd learned her lesson. "He's not the same man I knew."

"You'll find him again," Alberta said.

Trudie shook her head. "I'm not so sure." The more important part was she wasn't sure she wanted to, not in that way. She didn't relish another dose of heartbreak and hurt.

"I've seen them together and I've seen the two of you together. Trust an old matchmaker on this."

Tansy nodded in agreement. "Usually something cataclysmic occurs and things shift."

"That happened when his grandmother died," Alberta said. "I sense an equally important change now."

They weren't listening to her, so Trudie said it again. "I don't know him anymore."

"One way to fix that..." Alberta said with a smirk. "Get to know him again."

"Funny, that's what he said."

"I vote for that plan of action as well," Tansy said.

"We all seem to forget he's got a girlfriend," Trudie reminded them.

"I wouldn't be too sure of that," Alberta said. "You might want to try asking him. I'm not convinced." She smirked.

"But he's here with her."

"I still say just ask."

"I second that strategy," Tansy said, sipping at a cup of tea.

"What, is this relationship by committee?" Trudie asked.

Alberta grinned unabashedly. "Absolutely. Sometimes falling in love takes a village."

Tansy smiled. "Well, speaking from the voice of experience, Good Riddance is just the village for that job."

5

"CAN YOU GET that branch? The one...right there, a little to
the right.... Perfect."

Knox glanced down at Trudie from where he was perched
in a spruce tree, fetching the perfect branch for her. She'd
gone with him to the bison ranch earlier. Now he was helping
her collect the "materials" for her floral decorations.

Her blue-and-green striped knit cap bore a dusting of snow.
In the waning light, her cheeks were rosy.

He could swear the sun was brighter, the snow whiter, and
the air sweeter today than it had been in a really long time.
And he'd been excruciatingly aware of her all day—the way
her eyes sparkled, her scent, her warmth. It was as if he was
in the grips of a fever. As agreed, he'd escorted Elsa to dinner last night, but he'd had little patience with her demands
and chatter.

Trudie, the thought of Trudie, his desire for Trudie, had
been a constant ache. He'd tossed and turned through a sleepless night, wanting another kiss, wanting her. In his fevered
brain, he'd made love to her numerous times, numerous ways
throughout the night. However, the ache was still with him.
It had actually intensified as the day wore on.

He made the cut and handed the branch down to her. Even

Jessup had caught the fever, although the dog's was more holiday excitement. Jessup had set aside his snow aversion and was rolling around in the white stuff like a maniac.

"Your dog has lost his mind," Trudie said, laughing at his antics.

Knox knew the feeling. "Maybe. But he seems pretty content."

"He's making canine snow angels."

"If you say so."

"I do."

Knox hadn't known what a snow angel was until Trudie had explained it to him the first winter he'd lived with Mormor. His grandmother would be happy that he and Trudie were hanging out together again.

"Thanks for coming with me this morning," he said.

Trudie trudged through the drift to add the new branch to her collection in his truck bed. "Are you kidding? That was so cool." She returned to the tree. "Just to see the operation and the setup was awesome."

They'd flown into the bison ranch just as the sun was inching up over the horizon. The shaggy beasts had stood in majestic contrast to the white landscape. "It was a sight to behold, wasn't it? All the bison against the snow?"

The whine of snowmobiles sounded in the distance. A chickadee fussed noisily one tree over. The faint scent of wood smoke punctuated the cold air.

"Yeah, it was pretty incredible. Thanks for inviting me. Dwight was really nice."

Well, just how damn nice did she think he was? Jealousy knotted low in Knox's gut. What the hell was wrong with him? First off, he'd known a moment of the green-eyed monster when Trudie had talked about going fishing with that Jeremy whatever his name was and then she'd seemed to smile a lot at Dwight, the bison ranch owner, today.

So? She was a free agent...and a damn nice person...and a damn pretty woman and smart and fun to boot, so why wouldn't she be looking? And why wouldn't Dwight or her new fishing buddy or any other guy be looking back? And it seemed to Knox that Dwight had definitely been interested. Not that the rancher had been out of line or acted a fool, but a man knew when another man found a woman attractive.

It had never been a problem for Knox before, but he suddenly found that it was—a big load of a problem.

He wanted her. She'd been there all along, right in front of him, and he'd been too stupid and too blind to see. Now he saw, but was he too late? Was she willing to really know him again? Would she want him as a man, as a lover, not simply as a friend? Despite the explosiveness of last night's kiss, or perhaps because of it, she'd been friendly, but guarded, today.

"You gonna stay up there all day or what?" she said with a cheeky smile.

"Smartass." Knox laughed. "Maybe I will just stay up here for a while."

"Suit yourself. I'll wait in the truck because I've got some sense." She grinned in the direction of his vehicle parked on the side of the road. "But feel free to sit up there and freeze your butt off."

He dropped to the ground with a thunk, the deep snow cushioning the impact. Nonetheless, it threw his balance off. He reached for the first thing in front of him—Trudie—at the same time she reached out to steady him.

Knox fell backwards into the snow. Trudie landed on top of him. All the air seemed to leave his lungs. It wasn't the impact of the fall, but the press of her against him. Her eyes widened and her lips parted. Her warm, fragrant breath mingled with his. Her lower body pressed intimately against his. Want...need...hunger...arced between them, bound them.

He was lying in a bed of snow and he was on fire for her. He'd wanted just this thing all day.

"Trudie…" He wrapped his arms around her, securing her even tighter and harder against him.

"Knox…" she seemed to breathe his name on her exhale. He could swear he felt her heart racing against his chest through the layers of their clothes and jackets, which was just plain damn crazy…almost as crazy as what he was about to do…what they were about to do.

He cupped the back of her head in his gloved hand. She might say she didn't want them to kiss again but she damn sure wasn't making any move to get up. He pulled her head down to his. The smoke of their breath mingled as she drew closer. Her warm breath gusted against his face. The rest was up to her—what she really wanted was about to be known. His hand still rested against the back of her head but those last few inches—it was up to her to bridge them.

He looked into her eyes. Her dark pupils mirrored him. He opened himself to her, letting her see how much he wanted her. He also let her see his uncertainty.

Their lips were cold but the kiss was hot. The cold began to seep away until there was only heat and her soft pliant mouth meeting his.

This time it was Trudie teasing her tongue against his lips, seeking entry. He groaned and pulled her closer as her tongue swiped against his. Fire licked through him, between them.

Nothing else existed for him. It was simply the feel of her, the fit of her curves against his body, the press of her pelvis between his thighs, her taste, the reverberation of her moans, the velvet stroke of her tongue.

And it wasn't enough. It wasn't nearly enough. Frantic need pulsed through him. He wanted to know her intimately. He wanted her naked in his bed where he could explore the texture of her skin with his hands, his mouth, know the taste of every inch of her, hear her moan his name in the throes of passion. He wanted to see her eyes alight with a fire stoked by him and subsequently quenched by him. He wanted her—all of her—every inch of her. Fire...want...need...consumed him.

A sudden loud barking startled them apart. Jessup stood staring at them, apparently unsure if they were okay, definitely baffled by Trudie on top of Knox and the moaning and groaning going on.

Trudie raised her head, breaking the kiss, pushing away from Knox. He loved his dog, but this was twice now....

She scrambled to her feet, visibly shaken. Knox staggered upright as well, feeling drunk from kissing her. His legs weren't quite steady beneath him and it didn't have a damn thing to do with the cold. Conversely, it was all about the heat.

Trudie looked at him, panic flaring in her eyes, her lips full and red from their kisses. "Why did you... We shouldn't... That was a mistake."

They might go down a path, but it wasn't going to be that one. "No, it wasn't. It was a lot of things, but it was not a damn mistake."

She couldn't have changed that much in the last year and a half. The woman he knew didn't kiss casually and she damn sure wouldn't have kissed him with that kind of passion if it wasn't what she was feeling. Some women kissed by rote—like the paint-by-number kits they'd used as kids. The picture didn't really matter, you just filled in the blank with the color listed.

He had finally figured out Elsa operated that way. Their relationship had never been personal, which made breaking up all the easier to do. She hadn't particularly seemed to care when he told her he didn't want to see her anymore. Elsa required a passably attractive man at her beck and call. Hence, she'd wanted Knox to accompany her to Good Riddance. It really had nothing to do with him—he was just the color needed to fill in the blank spot on the canvas.

That, however, was not the way Trudie operated. She didn't simply make out for the sake of doing it. Everything with Trudie was personal. So, when she kissed him like that, when he felt the press of her thighs against his, it wasn't just blind lust speaking, but desire for *him*. There might not be a hell of a lot that he did know about her these days, but he knew that much with unwavering certainty.

Trudie wrapped her arms around her middle and for a second he thought she'd turn her back to him. She didn't. She faced him, eyes flashing.

"It was a mistake for any number of reasons but first and foremost because you have a girlfriend and I don't sneak around kissing some other woman's man behind her back."

Knox caught the shimmer of tears in Trudie's eyes. He didn't know if they were tears of frustration or anger or self-loathing, but the one thing he damn well couldn't stand was the thought of Trudie crying when he could so easily change that for her. To hell with blowing Elsa's "cover." He'd put her before Trudie once before, laid his loyalties in a way that had hurt Trudie, and he'd be damned if he'd hurt her that way again.

"I'm not Elsa's man," he said.

"Right." Arms still wrapped around her middle, she turned her back to him.

He approached her rigid form, lightly putting his hands on her shoulders, turning her to face him once again.

"Trudie, I know I've hurt you but you know I've never been a liar…or a player. How I feel about Elsa aside, I would never disrespect you that way—making you a side dish. And I'm not made that way. I wouldn't kiss you if I was still involved with Elsa."

Wariness gleamed in her eyes. "Then why are you here

with her? This isn't making any sense. Help me understand what's going on here because I'm confused and I just don't need this." She took a step away, shrugging off his touch.

"I told Elsa over a week ago that it was over." He shoved his hands in his pants pockets. "She took it well enough, but she had this gig coming up and asked me to escort her." He shrugged because it really hadn't been a big deal and he'd been ready to come back to Chrismoose. "I wanted to come anyway. It was short notice for her to find someone else. I agreed to escort her and keep my mouth shut so the whole town wouldn't be buzzing with our breakup."

Her lower lip trembled and more tears shimmered in her eyes before she looked away from him. Puzzled, he rubbed the back of his neck with his gloved hand. He didn't know what it was, but something had just gone terribly wrong. This was not the reaction he'd expected. "What's wrong?"

"So, you told her more than a week ago that you and she were done?"

Why did Trudie sound pissed about that? He'd have thought it would've been a good thing in her book. He really, seriously, just didn't understand the way a woman's mind worked sometimes—old friend or not. "Yeah. And you've never liked her anyway so why are you acting all crazy over that?"

"Crazy?" Her voice rose an octave. Maybe that hadn't been the best choice of word. "Really?" Okay, no *maybe* to it. Definitely not the best choice of wording. Note to self—don't use the term *crazy* in conjunction with Trudie's behavior again—even if it did seem spot-on. "You break up with her, don't even contact me, I'm not even on your freaking radar, but then I show up here and hey, you think I'm some convenient rebound material? It's not like you went out of your way to find me. It's just like, hey, why not make out with good old Trudie since she's handy."

"Trudie, it's not like that."

"That's what it seems like. No call, no nothing."

He'd thought about it. He'd actually considered picking up the phone or sending her a text but he'd known she'd be here. He'd known they were bound to run into one another. It had just seemed easier not to call or text, so he hadn't. Apparently, that was the wrong course of action.

"You just run into me and you think I'm easy because we have history. You can kiss my ass, Knox Whitaker."

She was so cute with her eyes flashing, telling him off, and he quipped the first thing that came to mind. "I'd like to, I'm trying."

Her mouth temporarily dropped open and for a second he thought she might laugh, might defuse. Instead it went the other way and her eyes blazed with fury. She opened her mouth, no doubt to rip him a new one, and he jumped in ahead of her.

"Okay. Sorry. That wasn't funny, I guess. I was just trying to make you laugh."

"I'm not laughing."

"Yeah, I noticed."

"Stay away from me. Obviously we aren't going to be the friends we were before and obviously you don't have enough respect for me to treat me like a woman you're interested in deserves to be treated. I am not some old shoe you can just slip back on."

"Dammit, Trudie. I don't think of you as an old shoe."

"Then, dammit, Knox, don't treat me like one. You can take me home now."

They climbed in the truck and tension stretched between them like taut barbed wire. Even Jessup wore a mournful expression. Once again, Knox knew how he felt.

At last he pulled up in front of the cabin Trudie was staying in. Silently he helped her transfer the greenery they'd collected to her SUV.

He should leave. Instead he lingered on the front porch. He knew now he'd screwed up a year and a half ago. Apparently he was still screwing up. He didn't want to keep doing it.

He started to put his hands on her shoulders but stopped himself. The truth of the matter was he wanted to touch her too bad and he wasn't sure that he could simply put his hands on her shoulders without pulling her into his arms again. He shoved his hands in his pockets instead.

"You told me to stay away from you. You also said I'm not respecting you so I'm going to ask you point blank if what you really want is for me to keep away. It's not what I want. I don't *think* it's what you want. But if it is, then I'll leave you alone."

She wrapped her arms around her middle and looked away from him. "You walked out of my life once before. Apparently it was easy for you. It nearly killed me. I don't want to go through that again. I *can't*...I *won't* go through that again. Do you understand what I'm saying?"

He wasn't sure, but he knew how desperate he felt not to let her go. "I think so."

"Figure out why you didn't call me when you knew you were done with Elsa."

"Dammit, Trudie...." This time he did put his hands on her shoulders.

She shrugged off his touch. "Save it, Knox."

He knew this mood. It was time to retreat and regroup. He had some things to figure out.

He whistled under his breath as he pulled out of her drive. She'd said lots of things, but she hadn't said that she wanted him to leave her alone. He still stood a chance.

6

TRUDIE COCKED her head to one side and adjusted the berries in the arrangement. "What do you think?" she asked Merrilee.

They were in the community center at the end of town. The chinked-log building would host many of the Chrismoose events from the cook-off to the Miss Chrismoose pageant. Five minutes ago it had been buzzing with people doing this and that, getting ready for tomorrow's kickoff. Trudie had spent the afternoon putting together small arrangements for each table.

The scent of fresh greenery perfumed the air and clung to her hands. But it was the taste of Knox's kiss that lingered on her lips, the press of his hardness between her thighs that left her aching and wanting and so confused she couldn't think straight. She'd hoped to lose herself in work, but that hadn't quite happened.

Merrilee and Trudie had the place to themselves now. No doubt, at any minute, someone would walk in the door.

Merrilee eyed Trudie. "I think you're miserable. You want to talk about it? Of course it's fine if you don't."

Trudie shrugged and stood, then walked over to the window. Lights from the makeshift camp at the outskirt of town punctuated the dark. She felt as if she was about to burst inside but if she started talking she wasn't sure she could stop.

Merrilee spoke behind her. "Knox?"

Trudie turned to face the other woman. "Of course." She paused at the table next to the window to tweak the spruce branch around the votive candle to a better angle.

"You know whatever you want or need to talk about won't go any further than here." For the most part news spread around Good Riddance like butter in a hot skillet. Trudie did know, however, that Merrilee could keep a confidence.

Merrilee had known both Knox and her since they were children, but she wasn't family and she wasn't one of Trudie's personal girlfriends. She was more of a neutral friend.

Trudie sank into the chair opposite Merrilee and it was like ice breaking on the river during a spring thaw. The words and emotions tumbled out of her. All of it—the hurt, the abandonment, the betrayal, the anger...and the fear.

Merrilee touched the back of her hand lightly. "Oh, honey, I've watched the two of you over the years and I've known you were in love with him for a long time."

"You did? How could you know when I didn't?"

"Sometimes we're too close to our own situation to see it clearly."

"That's a little mortifying. I'm sure half the town knows, too. So, is everyone watching to see if I'm broken-hearted over Knox and Elsa?"

Merrilee offered an eyebrow shrug. "I'm not going to lie— of course people talk but it really doesn't matter, does it?" Trudie didn't suppose that it did. "The most important person is totally unaware. Knox doesn't seem to know."

"Knox is an idiot," Trudie said, giving vent to her frustration. "And the worst of it is, I still love him. I'm still in love with him."

It was such a relief to just say it, to throw it out there. She hadn't been able to talk about her relationship with Knox to her mother because her mother was already worried about him. Trudie didn't need her mother worrying about her as well. And all of Trudie's friends were beyond disgusted with him over the way he'd fallen for Elsa's cool beauty and dumped his friendship with Trudie. She'd learned to keep her mouth shut around them when it came to her feelings for him. They'd told her repeatedly she needed to get over him and move on. They said she deserved better if he couldn't recognize what a jewel she was. She had the feeling, however, that Merrilee would understand in a way her friends didn't. Merrilee had lived a lot longer.

"I don't know how to *not* love him. It's not like it's some spigot you can just turn off and on."

"Truer words were never spoken. Love can be both a curse and a blessing, can't it?"

"I'm not seeing much blessing here." She shook her head. Her feelings seemed so helplessly out of her control. "I'm angry and I don't want to be hurt like that again. He just walked away from me, from our friendship. If we take it further now and he pulls away again…I don't know how I'll survive." How much could a woman take? She didn't want to be put to the test. "And he broke up with Elsa and didn't even call me. All this time, I blamed Elsa, even though Knox always had a choice. We all have choices, but it was easier to blame her. But he didn't call me," she repeated, "even when they broke up."

Merrilee didn't hesitate. "He's embarrassed."

Trudie considered Merrilee's assessment for a second, pursing her lips. She wasn't seeing it. "He doesn't seem embarrassed. He just wants to act like the last year and a half never happened—let's just sweep it under the rug."

Merrilee made a noise that sounded suspiciously like a snort. "Of course he wants to sweep it under the rug. He was hurting—he was grieving—and he hurt you. Why would he want to talk about it? Trust me on this. And as you just said, everyone has choices. So, look at your choices and make one."

"I'm—" Trudie faltered.

"Scared," Merrilee finished for her.

"Yes."

"That's because love is scary territory. It's not easy. It's complicated and simple all at the same time." The older woman gave a sage nod. "And with or without it, life steamrollers on. Regardless of which choice you make, you're still going to wake up tomorrow. Chrismoose is still going to unfold. You'll still have your job, unless you choose to do something different. Whether that life includes Knox in it or not, well, that seems to be your choice. Decide whether your life is better with him or without him, but..."

"There's always a but, isn't there?"

"Life is all about the buts, sweetie. And the but here is you can let Knox back into your life, definitely your choice, but the only thing you can control is you. You can lay ground rules but you know there's no guarantee."

"What if we sleep together and it's awful?"

Merrilee laughed. "Do you really think it's going to be awful?"

Trudie knew she was grasping at straws. Kissing Knox was unlike kissing anyone else. It had been fireworks and shooting stars and magic—both times. It had been even better than she'd imagined. How would kissing anyone else ever measure up? And if that's what kissing was like, making love with him would probably totally ruin her for any other man. "Uh, no, I don't really think so."

"Honey, I don't think so either. But if it is, then it is. What's worse, the experience being awful or just never knowing and spinning out some what-if or if-only fantasy?" Merrilee summed it up. "You love him."

"I do, but I'm afraid to trust him emotionally."

"I don't know what to tell you about that except he's not the kind of guy who would deliberately hurt you. It would simply be ignorance on his part, not callousness."

"I don't know. He's seemed pretty callous the last year and a half."

"I think he was numb." Trudie's face must have reflected her skepticism. Merrilee smiled. "And no, I'm not taking up for him. Everyone grieves differently. I think Knox was so drowning in grief he didn't know what to do."

That especially made no sense to Trudie. "But I was his best friend. Why didn't he talk to me?" She realized that was a huge part of the betrayal. Why hadn't he confided in her, sought comfort and solace in her rather than pushing her away?

"I think that was precisely the problem. I think it was so raw and painful he didn't want to talk about it or think about it, and if he was with you, he almost had to. You were part of his history with Mormor and I'm sure being around you dredged up lots of memories and emotions. He probably wasn't ready to deal with any of it, so it was easier to simply walk away."

Trudie listened. It was so different from what she'd thought for some time now. "But it's almost as if Elsa had him under a spell...."

"You've got to keep looking for him, Trudie. Knox is still in there, you just have to keep looking."

KNOX SQUARED his shoulders outside the spa at the end of town. The place hadn't been here the last time he was in town. He was entering foreign territory but a man had to do what a man had to do. He opened the door and stepped inside.

"How can I help you?" A pretty blonde woman who bore

a very startling resemblance to a Barbie doll sat behind the reception desk.

The place was nice. A waterfall cascaded behind the desk. The quiet, soothing notes of native flute music interspersed with the sounds of birds drifted on the air, imparting a sense of tranquility.

The name on the front of the woman's "lab coat" read Jenna.

"Hi, Jenna. I need a gift. Actually, I need several gifts."

"Sure. I can help you with that." She moved from behind the counter and led him to a display case. "How personal do you want it? Something generic like hand soap or something a little more personal like bath salts?"

Hell if he knew. "Uh..."

She laughed. "Okay, let's start here—girlfriend, sister or mother?"

And that question was supposed to make it easier? Trudie wasn't his sister or his mother, but he didn't know exactly what she was or wasn't in the other regards at this point. "She's not my mother or my sister, and I'm not sure about the girlfriend business. I guess that's why I need the presents."

She smiled encouragingly, understanding glinting in her eyes. Knox wavered. He'd love to talk to another woman about Trudie, but he'd agreed to keep his status with Elsa quiet. He made a split decision. He'd put Elsa and her dictates ahead of Trudie for the last time. There was no dishonor in him escorting Elsa as a platonic friend. It was certainly a more honest presentation of what they were.

"We were friends and I never really saw her as anything more than that. We drifted apart but now I want to be friends again, no...I want to be more than friends. The problem is she's pretty unhappy about the last year and a half..."

"Ah. You must be Knox Whitaker."

He'd known when he started yapping that he was in a

small town where nothing stayed quiet long, so he was only mildly disconcerted that she'd "made" him so immediately. "Yeah, I am."

A woman he didn't recognize walked in. "Excuse me," Jenna said to Knox. "I'll be right back." She greeted the woman with a big, genuine smile. "Lola Dane?"

"That's me."

"Come right on back. We're ready for you." Jenna led the woman down the hall but within a minute or two she returned.

"Okay. So...where were we? Gifts for a friend who used to be a friend and isn't happy with you." She laughed. "I take it this isn't for Elsa."

Elsa had had a session at the spa either today or yesterday. He wasn't particularly keeping up with her schedule. "Uh...no."

"Trudie Brown?"

In another place he might've resented the prying, but hey, this was Good Riddance, so what did it matter?

"Yeah, it's for Trudie. We've always given one another little gifts each day until Christmas. It started when we were kids with that 'Twelve Days of Christmas' song. We were apart last year. Now we're both here but I don't have anything for her. I need twelve gifts."

Jenna nodded. "What's her favorite color? Her favorite scent?"

"Her favorite color is blue. She's a florist, so she likes flower scents, particularly roses, and her favorite color of rose is that sort of orange/yellow one."

"Well, that makes sense, huh? Okay, give me a minute."

Jenna began pulling things off the shelves. When she had a little pile she turned to him. "What do you think? We could wrap them individually. A candle, bath salts, relaxing flute music, a scented lotion, bath mitt, rose essential oil, and a skin-care kit. I keep some spa robes in the back, and of course, we offer gift certificates. And because we cater to women, we also carry a line of chocolates. And I have some hand-crafted jewelry."

"That all sounds great. I'd like to see the jewelry."

"Absolutely."

She led him to a display case on the opposite wall. He didn't know much about jewelry but it looked like nice stuff. There was native beading and a selection of necklaces, brace-lets and earrings crafted in metals. He was more drawn to the metals.

In particular a ring caught his eye. It was a wide band with a flower bloom on top. The bloom was delicate, ready to un-furl. It made him want to watch its progression. He immediately thought of Trudie.

"I'd like to take a closer look at that," he said, pointing to the ring.

"It's beautiful, isn't it?" Jenna took it out, eyeing it.

He held the ring between two fingers. It was well crafted. He'd even go so far as to say exquisite.

He handed it back to Jenna. "I'll take it. And if you can throw in a gift certificate for the works. And wrap up one of those robes you were talking about."

"You want to wait or you want to drop by later to pick it up? It'll take a little bit to wrap it all individually."

"I'll come back in…what do you think, maybe an hour?"

"That works. Do you want sticky notes for what's in each box or does it matter?"

"How about I number them and then you can just put the number on the back of the box?"

"Okey dokey."

Within a few minutes he'd assigned each item a number.

Jenna nodded, offering him an approving smile. "She'll love all of it."

He was counting on that…but mostly he wanted her to

know how much she meant to him…although he wasn't altogether sure that he knew himself. He did, however, know she meant a lot.

Now that she'd been out of his life, he realized how much better it was with Trudie in it.

7

IF SHE HADN'T left the front porch light on, she might've tripped over the gifts on her doorstep. But she had left it on, and she didn't trip over the packages.

Her heart flip-flopped in her chest because she knew the bow-topped boxes were from Knox. They had to be. Who else would've left it for her?

Excitement and anticipation welled up within her as she picked them up. She'd so missed their gift exchange last year. It seemed every store window she passed, every ad she saw, she thought of him. Even when she was internet surfing, she'd find things she knew he'd like.

Balancing her boxes in one arm, she went into the chilly cabin. They'd always opened the gifts together. Trudie knew they were more than just presents.

It was a return to tradition—it was also a calling card. She placed the packages on the table and crossed to the stove. She hesitated. Did she want to crank up the heat with Knox? If she accepted his gifts, she was accepting far, far more than what was beneath that fancy wrapping.

Yes. She wanted it. She wanted him. For tonight, she'd have him on her terms. They'd make that leap from friends to lovers and hope they both stayed intact. And either way it went, she wouldn't bring regrets to the table.

Heat and desire coursed through her. She'd wanted him, dreamed of his touch. That light in his eyes she'd seen today... she should be nervous. Instead she simply felt in the grips of something hot and heavy inside her. Anticipation tightened her skin, tingled between her thighs.

She picked up her cell phone and rang him. It rolled to voice mail and disappointment flooded her. She plopped onto the sofa. She hadn't considered him not answering. What now? It was incredibly anticlimactic, but she supposed she could hang up her half of the ornaments she and Knox had made as kids. She'd assembled the tree the night before but hadn't gotten around to decorating. Nah.

She wandered over to the kitchen, opened the refrigerator then closed the door again. Nothing in there looked particularly appealing. She could— The text notification went off on her cell phone. She crossed the room in record time.

With Elsa now at function. Hour and a half work for you?

Jealousy, swift and hot, knifed through her. He'd make time for her when he was done with Elsa? She drew a deep breath and reminded herself that Knox was here as Elsa's escort. And he wanted to spend the evening with Trudie after his public obligations were met. Knox was making a choice here. Trudie made her choice. She texted back.

C u then.

Her heart raced. An hour and a half? She'd drive herself insane before then. She'd have to stay busy.

An hour and a half later she'd finished decorating the tree, showered, and dressed. She'd just dragged the brush through her hair again, when he texted.

On my way.

Ten minutes later she heard the pull of his truck engine. There was no point in prevarication. She had the door opened by the time he turned the engine off.

Jessup leaped out of the cab and bounded up the steps. Knox followed in a more orderly fashion. He hesitated at her door. Trudie hesitated as well. To kiss or not to kiss? The moment passed as he followed the dog in.

Trudie closed the door behind them. With a smile he shrugged out of his jacket. Good Lord, he smelled good... and he looked even better. He wore a greenish-gray zip-up sweater with heavy trousers. It suited him—dressy, yet casual.

It took her a hot minute to realize he looked and smelled good...to escort Elsa. The insight didn't totally ruin the moment for Trudie, but it took an edge off her glow.

"How'd it go tonight?" she said. "You look nice." And that was an understatement. He was knee-weakeningly handsome and heat-inducingly sexy. She should've kissed him when he came in.

He shrugged. "It was okay. You know I'm not really into all of that. I would've been here a little earlier but I stopped by the cabin to change and pick up Jessup. You don't mind that I brought him, do you? He's been alone all afternoon and I wasn't..." he suddenly seemed as unsure of himself as she felt "...well, I wasn't sure how long I might be over here this evening."

"It was fine to bring him. He's always welcome." She felt the smile wreathing her face. She was still stuck back on the fact that he wasn't just looking sharp because he'd escorted Elsa. He'd changed for her, Trudie.

He studied her and the expression in his eyes left her breath in her chest. "Good Lord, you're beautiful, Trudie."

A flush rolled through her, leaving a dampness between her thighs. She was glad she'd opted for the long black skirt that flared slightly from the knees down and the low-cut black top shot through with threads of gold and silver. She'd brought it to wear to the Miss Chrismoose pageant but decided it could pull double duty. The expression in his eyes said it had been a good decision on her part.

Suddenly she didn't know where to look, but she found she couldn't sustain contact with that heated gaze without totally melting. She glanced away from him as she said, "Thanks."

Knox nodded toward the tree in the corner. "I see you got your tree up. It looks nice."

Tension stretched between them like a fishing line with a salmon on the other end.

He shoved his hands in his pant pockets. "So, you want to open your presents?"

Yes. And she wanted to kiss him…and be kissed by him…. All in good time.

"I don't have yours." She'd thought about it but she'd been busy and then she found she just wasn't ready to take that step.

"It's fine, Trudie." He grinned and her world seemed to turn upside down. "And you do have a gift for me—you're accepting these, so…." He scooped one up from beneath the tree where she'd placed them, and held it out her. "Open it."

"Okay." Her fingers brushed his as she took the package. That brief contact shot through her, rocking her.

Her hands weren't quite steady as she tore into the paper, tossing aside the bow. Knox leaned against the wall, watching her. He'd watched her for nearly twenty Christmases, but this time felt different. "I've always loved the way you open presents—you just rip into them."

She returned his smile as she tossed aside the paper. "Is there any other way?"

It was a candle, but not just any candle. It had been hand-crafted and Alaskan wildflowers were pressed into the thick pillar.

She held it to her nose and inhaled. The faint aroma of the dried flowers was there. It smelled as good as it looked. "It's lovely. Thank you." Okay, she had to ask. "Did you pick it out?"

He ran his hand over his head, a sheepish expression on his face. Knox was a notoriously awful gift-buyer. Mormor had always helped him choose Trudie's gifts. "Not exactly. I gave final approval but Jenna at the spa did the picking."

"Oh, good. That means they'll be nice, not weird."

"You're never going to let me live down the travel sewing kit, are you?"

She laughed. He'd given her a travel sewing kit for her birthday one year. "Nope."

Rolling his eyes, he handed her the second gift. Lavender bath salts. "Thank you. I love it."

He took a step toward her, his intent clear in the glimmer in his eyes. With a shocking disregard for her presents, she put the bath salts on the table next to her candle, her interest caught and held by his advance.

He opened his arms and she walked into his embrace. Her heart tattooing a rhythm, she simply stood there for a moment, absorbing him as his arms closed about her, pulling her into intimate contact. His heat...his strength...his scent... She rested her head against his chest and wound her arms around him, her fingers seeking his taut back muscles through his sweater. Languor replaced the frantic longing she'd known earlier.

Knox reached between them and tilted her chin up with one finger, a question in his eyes but no words coming from his lips. Maintaining the same silence, she answered him with her own eyes. He gave a slight nod of satisfaction as she slid her hand up to cup the nape of his neck with her palm.

Somewhere in the room, the dog sighed and the firewood snapped and popped. His lips descended on hers. She leaned up a bit.

Those earlier kisses hadn't been an aberration, and this one was even more potent and delicious. It became a litany of long, slow, clinging kisses that explored, celebrated, and turned her on in a way she'd never been turned on before.

And then it was as if they were both making up for lost time. Their kisses stoked a deep, drugging heat that tore through her and reached into her soul, nurturing the part of her that had hungered for him for so long.

Somehow they wound up on the couch and he hesitated, his hand nearly touching her breast but not quite there. She was very much aware that heated kisses were one thing but intimate touching was something altogether different. She cupped her hand around the back of his and moved his palm to cover her breast.

He moaned into her mouth and she returned the sentiment with a long vocal sigh that she couldn't have stopped if she wanted to…and she didn't want to. His touch felt so good. It was just flesh against flesh but this time was different, special…and incredibly arousing. Her nipple hardened against his palm and he dragged his mouth from hers. He scattered kisses along the column of her neck. He nuzzled and nibbled as he palmed and smoothed his fingers over her skin. She pushed her breast into his palm, aching for his firm touch… his wet mouth….

It was as if he read her mind. He nuzzled the flesh at the top of her bra and her head dropped back. He nudged her bra aside and then her nipple was in his mouth. It was as if all the planets in the universe lined up or collided in some astonishing cosmic event. Any semblance of holding back, of maintaining distance and control, was forgotten.

Much as she'd done with the present earlier, she tore at Knox's packaging, dispensing with his sweater and the long-sleeved undershirt in record time. She didn't hesitate at his belt, speedily unbuckling and then unzipping his pants.

He stood, his chest heaving. She'd seen him in a swimsuit more times than she could count but this was different.

There was an intimacy, a sexuality in his bare chest and belly, his unzipped pants that had never existed between them before. "Bedroom?" he said, holding out his hand.

"Yes," she said, putting her palm in his. He threaded his fingers through hers. They both knew her *yes* covered so much more than simply a trip to the other room. It was an opportunity for her to change her mind, to opt out of taking their relationship to the next level—of establishing a new relationship in territory they'd never ventured into before. It was a yes to them as lovers and not simply friends.

Light from the den spilled into the bedroom. Neither of them turned on the lamp.

As Knox began to unlace his boots, Trudie sat on the edge of the bed and unabashedly watched. He stepped out of the boots, then his socks. She'd always loved the shape of his feet. How crazy goofy was that?

The silence between them thickened, deepened as he pulled a cellophane-wrapped condom out of his pocket and placed it on the bedside table. It might have been a mood breaker, but it wasn't in the least.

He hooked his thumbs in the top of his pants and tugged them down. She stood, drawing her fingernail down his chest and the flat plane of his belly until it rested at the top of his boxers. "I'd like to do the honors."

"Do with me what you will, Trudie," he said, offering her himself.

She caught the elastic band with one finger and tugged the cotton down, over the jut of his erection. "Oh," she said in the semi-dark room. All the daydreaming and fantasizing she'd done was inadequate preparation for the reality of Knox Whitaker naked...for her...with her. Bemused, she trailed her finger down his rigid length.

"Trudie..." he said.

She leaned forward and pressed a kiss to a spot above his hip. She inhaled his scent and the feel of his skin against hers, the pulse of his erection against her palm. He tangled his fingers in her hair and the sound of their breathing filled the room.

Gently, he urged her upward and she went. Wordlessly, he undressed her—skirt, top, bra and panties. And then he stepped back and looked at her. It took everything within her not to wrap her arms around her to hide her nakedness. It felt as much a baring of the soul as a baring of the flesh.

He nodded, still not speaking. But it was a good nod. She sank to the edge of the mattress, her thighs and buttocks embraced by the brushed flannel sheets. Bracing one knee next to her, Knox gentled Trudie down. She sank back into the mattress. He eased his weight next to hers.

For a moment, Trudie thought about pinching herself but his heat, his weight, the press of his leg against hers, the rush of his breath stirring her hair were all very real.

Knox's touch was gentle as he teased his fingertips over the curve of her shoulder, along her collarbone. Heat suffused her. Trudie sighed and rolled to face him, bringing her body into intimate contact with his. She bit her lip as she pressed her nipples against the hair-roughened plane of his chest. The sensation shot straight through to her vagina.

She explored him. Kissed the column of his neck while she touched his penis, reveling in the velvety, rigid length, the weight of his balls. He was thicker and longer than she'd anticipated.

She sat up and looked down at him in the half-light cast from the other room. He was beautiful. Solid and trim and wonderful.

He reached up and gentled his hand over her cheeks. "Do I want to know what you're thinking?"

It was an invitation to share but she just wanted to hug her thoughts to herself for the moment. Instead she said, "It's all good."

Getting on her knees, she knelt over him and licked and kissed her way to his flat belly. She paused, his erection nudging her cheek, to inhale deeply. It was a potent combination—male arousal and the scent that had always been uniquely his. She licked at his inner thigh and he caught her head. "No, that tickles."

Unperturbed, she trailed her tongue along the length of his erection. He was like warm velvet and she teased the tip with her tongue. "Does that tickle?"

"Uh, no, but much more and I'll be finished before we get started." Knox laughed as he caught her and hauled her back up to lie next to him.

Trudie laughed, too. She was glad to know she affected him that way. It was strange to lie in bed naked with a man she thought she'd known so well, and who knew her, and discover so many new things.

He pulled her more firmly against him. "Trudie—" he nuzzled the edge of her neck "—you feel so good, so right."

"So do you," she said.

He cupped one breast in his hand, rubbing his thumb over the nipple. She loved the feel of his hands on her, his scent. He circled harder and she moaned.

Knox immediately stopped. "Did I hurt you?"

"No," she murmured, "I like it. Do it again." She pressed a kiss to the warm satin of his shoulder and nipped him.

"Um, come here," he said, guiding her up a bit. He nibbled at the turgid nub and she hissed an indrawn breath.

"Knox..."

He captured her nipple in his mouth and suckled her and it was the most incredible sensation. "Yes," she panted. He sucked harder and at the same time reached between her thighs to tease his finger against her wet folds. She arched her back, eager for more. He did the same with the other breast while he played with her sex. Her last rational thought was that she was an instrument that had finally landed in the hands of its master. He stroked and nipped and teased until she was on the brink of exploding and then he dialed it all back.

And then he started again, working her up to a fevered pitch until she felt as if she would die if he didn't give her the release her body needed. She hovered on the brink...and yet again he pulled.

She fisted her hands in the sheets, her breath coming in ragged pants. She was frantic with desire for him. "Knox... please..."

"What do you want, Trudie?" His voice was husky with his own need.

"You...now...inside me."

He rolled away and she heard the crinkle of the cellophane. "Okay," he said.

She reached between them and smoothed her hand down the length of his shaft.

"Is that what you want?" he asked.

"Yes." She wrapped her arms around him and pulled him to her, rolling on her back and spreading her legs.

He rose up and cupped her wet folds in his hand. "Good. Because this is what I want."

Wordlessly she draped her legs over his shoulders in invitation. He nudged at her with his thick head, again and again, going a little deeper each time, until, as before, she was frantic to have him all the way inside. When she thought she might lose her mind with need, he buried his cock inside her.

"Ahh…" It was a sigh of pleasure, of fullness. She closed her eyes and absorbed the sensation.

Knox set up a slow but steady pace that notched her higher and higher, then he gained momentum, thrusting harder and faster. It was pure sensation when her release came and waves of satisfaction pulsed through her, around her, in her.

Knox's low, guttural moan joined her own as he came.

He collapsed onto the bed beside her and she felt almost as if she was having an out-of-body experience, floating outside herself.

"I love you, Trudie," he said quietly.

That brought her back to herself. Quickly.

She opened her mouth but the words stuck in her throat. She could say it to herself, she'd said it to Merrilee, but the words wouldn't come for him.

"You're important to me, Knox."

It was the best she could do.

8

A QUARTER HOUR later, having cleaned up and let the dog in and out for a potty break, Knox lay in the semi-dark with his arm around Trudie.

"I feel better than I've felt in a long, long time," he said, the dark inviting confidences. And it was the truth, even if it had been a bit awkward when he'd declared how he felt about her and she'd merely come back with how important he was or some such nonsense.

"Are you okay?" she asked quietly. She was talking about his grandmother. He knew precisely what she was asking.

He plied his fingertips over the soothing smoothness of her shoulder. "I'm getting there. It's one of those things where you don't even know what's going on at the time. Of course, hindsight's twenty-twenty, isn't it?"

"You want to talk about it?"

"I'm not sure what there is to say." And then it hit him that Trudie did sort of deserve an explanation of where his head had been. "For a long time I was just kind of running on autopilot. I thought if I didn't think about Mormor, if I kept myself busy and didn't go back to the house, her things, the people that were part of our lives like you and your folks, then I simply didn't have to face that she was gone. I could just bury my head in the sand, so to speak. It sounds stupid when I put it that way."

She curled her fingers around his and pressed a kiss to his chest. "No, it doesn't sound stupid at all."

Relief flowed through him. He was glad she felt that way. "Now...now, I suppose I'm ready to come to terms with things and move forward. It's funny, I thought I was moving forward but I was just treading water."

There was an odd comfort in saying the words aloud.

"Everyone has to deal with things in their own way, and if that's the way you had to cope, well, you had to do what you had to do."

Her hair was soft and silky against his finger. "I'm sorry I hurt you."

She gave him another one of those kisses to his chest that seemed to brand him as hers, which was fine with him. "Me, too, but you were hurting." She brushed the back of his hand with her fingertips.

"I was. There just wasn't a whole lot left of me for anyone else."

Trudie offered a small snort and propped herself up on one elbow. "The last time I checked, Elsa was fairly demanding."

Knox laughed quietly. "It's all superficial. Everything Elsa requires doesn't pull too much out of you. Does that make any sense?"

They had to discuss Elsa, to get her out of the way, because the specter of her was there with them whether she was mentioned or not. They might as well get her out in the open. Elsa wasn't an issue for him but he sensed she still was for Trudie, so he'd do whatever it took to convince this woman that she was the only one that mattered to him.

"Not really. How can she be superficially demanding?"

"With Elsa, you just have to show up and look good and tell her she looks good. And I'm not being unkind, I'm just being bluntly honest. You don't have to think about what you do and you don't have to feel deep down. There are no deep currents with Elsa—it's just a float downstream in shallow water. Does that make sense?"

He saw it on her face when everything finally fell into place for her. She understood that while he had chosen Elsa over her that evening in July, it hadn't really been a rejection of their friendship or of Trudie. His decision had been dictated by his grief, his need to shut down and shut out so he could process his pain.

He'd had to take time to heal. His actions had hurt Trudie and she'd have to have time to heal as well. He'd wait. He'd wait as long as he had to because he had never been so sure of anything as he was sure that the two of them were right for one another.

Something primal and animalistic rose in him. The need to claim his mate the way animals did. He kissed her on the neck and then nipped her. She let out a little yelp of surprise and then laughed low and sexy. "Does that mean you're not sleepy?"

"No. Sleeping wasn't what I had in mind yet."

"Hmm. Well, I seem to have caught a second wind as well." She turned her back to him and pressed close, rubbing her bare ass against his burgeoning erection. Knox grinned in the dark. He and Trudie had always been tuned in to one another about so many things, it didn't surprise him in the least that they shared a sexual wavelength as well. And while it wasn't a surprise, it was pretty damn awesome that not only was she thinking sex but they seemed to be thinking the same kind of sex.

He bit her lightly on her shoulder and she clamped her hand down on his bare ass, digging her fingers into him. "Yes."

Knox reached around her and played with her breasts. They weren't overly big but they were plump and round and her nipples were beautifully distended. The more he squeezed, kneaded, and plucked, the more she ground back into him. Neither of them said a word.

Trudie moved into an erotic kind of grinding, thrusting against him with her lush ass. The head of his cock would catch between her thighs, and she turned her head and nipped at him a couple of times. The more she thrust back, the harder he grew.

Both of them were panting as she rolled to her belly and up on her knees in one smooth motion. Dropping her shoulders down, she spread her knees, hiking her ass in the air. Even in the half light, her sex glistened with arousal. She looked at him over her shoulder. Everything about her actions invited him to take her from behind.

His hands unsteady, he rolled on his last condom and mounted her. She was gloriously wet as she thrust back into him. She was so hot. It was a short, intense trip for both of them as he pounded into her and she threw it back at him.

Her cry mingled with his as they both came and then collapsed, still joined, on their sides.

This time the words weren't spoken but they reverberated in the room, nonetheless.

You belong to me.

KNOX SLEPT BETTER than he had in a really long time. He woke up to the press of Trudie against him. For a second he wondered if she was real or if he was dreaming—but she was warm, flesh-and-blood woman.

Oddly he hadn't realized until his discussion with Trudie just how shallow his relationship with Elsa had been. Elsa wanted to look good. She wanted him to look good. He needed to drive a late-model truck. They needed to be seen in "good" restaurants, vacation at high-end resorts. What he thought or felt wasn't an issue. And that wasn't a criticism. It simply was what it was.

He climbed out of bed and stoked the fire. It was cold in the cabin and Trudie would be up soon. Unless her habits had changed drastically, she wasn't one to sleep in. She might be hardy Alaskan stock, but Knox didn't want her to be cold.

He opened the front door to let Jessup out for his morning potty break. He started coffee and the dog scratched at the door, eager to come back in.

In a few minutes, Trudie poked her head around the door frame. Her hair was standing up on one side, mascara smudged beneath her eyes. She shouldn't have looked hot. Her bedhead and raccoon eyes shouldn't have made his heart thump against his ribs…but she did and they did. Unbidden, he thought he could wake up to this, to that, to her, for a long time to come.

"Morning." She lifted her nose into the air and sniffed, like a dog catching an airborne scent. "Do I smell coffee?"

Knox grinned up at her, altogether happy for this moment in time. Trudie's addiction to coffee was legendary. Really, it would take an intrepid or insane man, or a combination thereof, to spend time with her if she hadn't had her cup of joe in the morning. "I thought it was best not to risk my life."

"Wise man."

"I try. One sugar and two creams?"

"Yep. You got that right."

Ha. He thought about her moans of satisfaction, her noisy orgasm, and grinned. "Admit it. I got a lot right."

She wrinkled her nose, but grinned, nonetheless. "Don't get arrogant on me."

Knox prepared a cup for her and a cup for him. She'd disappeared from the doorway. "Hey, come get your coffee. It's ready."

"Come get it? Aren't you going to serve me in bed?" Amusement tinged her voice.

"Well, I've got to be in town in an hour and if you're in bed and I bring it up there...well, I'm not so sure that I'm going to leave on time." Now that he knew her in a different sense, well, it was impossible not to think of her, see her that way, want her. Lolling about in bed with a cup of coffee would inevitably lead to other activities that would throw him off-track.

"Okay," she groused, her smile belying her feigned grumpiness.

He handed her the cup and then reached up to smooth her hair down. His fingers lingered against the slight wave, the silky texture. Up close and personal, she smelled like a combination of Trudie his old friend and Trudie his new lover—her familiar shampoo and sex.

"So, I've been thinking," he said. He had a proposal for her. Nothing ventured, nothing gained.

"Scary," Trudie said, and then paused to take a sip of coffee. "Decent."

"Thanks."

"You've been thinking...." she prompted as she curled up on the end of the couch closest to the wood stove's warmth and tugged a tattered quilt over her. She was forever wanting to burrow under or next to something. Last night, it had been him.

"You could stay with me for the rest of Chrismoose."

She was quiet, staring into her coffee cup as if some secret was lurking in the dark depths. "I...I don't know."

"I see." He could read her body language, the withdrawal into herself.

She laughed but didn't sound particularly amused. "What is it that you see?"

What he saw was that he was pushing for too much too

soon. What he said, however, was altogether different. "That you're a traditionalist and you want to sleep in your own bed."

She sat there silent for so long he was beginning to think she wasn't going to answer. Finally she nodded slowly. "Busted." He wasn't exactly sure what was going on in her pretty head but she was about to lighten things up and that was fine. "You can go ahead and give me my next present if you want to."

He'd roll with the tone she set. "You're a shameless gift-grubber, Trudie Brown. How do you know I have another present for you?"

"Because if you gave me the first two, that means there are ten more to follow. There *are* more to follow, aren't there?"

"Since you're so eager to talk about presents...where are mine?"

"Patience, grasshopper. In due time. Meanwhile..." She held her hand out, palm up, expectantly.

"Gift-grubber."

"Of course. Now hand one over."

"It would serve you right if you didn't have anything else coming your way."

"Save the sermon." She glanced pointedly at the kitchen clock. "You've got to get ready to go soon."

Knox gave up and finally just laughed at her show of avarice. Trudie had always loved getting presents and it had never mattered whether they were expensive or not. Just hand over something wrapped in paper topped with a ribbon or a bow and she was a happy camper. It made him realize how much he'd missed her.

He crossed his arms over his chest. "You're behind by one present already. I'm holding out until you catch up. So, when I get my gift from yesterday...and the day before...then you'll get today's gift."

"Isn't it better to give than to receive?"

He was a guy and oral sex immediately came to mind. He damn near choked on his coffee. He pulled his mind out of the bedsheets and back to the matter at hand. Flirting with Trudie was fun. He'd have never had this conversation with Elsa primarily because Elsa didn't have Trudie's sense of humor or the capacity to poke fun at herself...and that was precisely what Trudie was doing, laughing at herself. And as for giving rather than receiving...

"Exactly, Ms. Brown. So where's my gift?"

Knox realized how relieved he was that even though they'd slept together they could still laugh and tease one another. He really hadn't known whether Trudie would get all flippy dippy on him once their relationship had taken a sexual turn.

"You'll get yours tonight," she said with a sultry look.

Yes, he would. And he was already looking forward to it.

TRUDIE FINISHED up her shopping for Knox. It hadn't been easy with so little to choose from, but she'd enjoyed the challenge.

Good Riddance was packed since it was the first day of Chrismoose. The dog sled races, one of her favorite events, was right after lunch. And she didn't even care that Elsa was officiating—the one to drop the flag and start the race. Trudie was still going.

For as much as Elsa had stuck in Trudie's craw for the last two years, now the woman simply didn't matter. Deep in thought, she was caught unawares when her mom linked her arm through the crook of Trudie's elbow. "Hey, there, stranger."

"Hi, Mom. You guys got here." Trudie looked over her mother's shoulder. "Where's Daddy?"

"He was heading over to Donna's." Donna's was a small-engine repair business that essentially had become a hang-out center for all things automotive. Donna had once upon a time been Don and no one seemed to care a whit. As Trudie's dad had said on more than one occasion, Donna had forgotten more than most men would ever know about engines so who gave a rat's ass if she was a chick who used to be a guy. "They're all doing last-minute things to get ready for the snowmobile races tomorrow. Men and their toys. Want to grab some lunch?"

"I'm starving!" She'd skipped breakfast and all of that amazingly great sex last night had left her famished. "Do you think we've got a chance to snag a table at Gus's?"

Her mother linked her arm through Trudie's and started down the sidewalk. "Oh, sure. The moose cook-off is going on down at the community center."

Trudie had been so wrapped up in present-buying—and thoughts of her incredible night with Knox—that she'd forgotten all about the cook-off. "Right."

"I'm thinking you've got a couple of other things besides a cook-off on your mind." Her mother's sly smile spoke volumes…but how could she know?

There weren't a ton of empty spots but Trudie and her mom managed to snag one…and that was, after all, all they needed.

Trudie didn't bother to look at the menu. She'd wanted pie since yesterday…day before yesterday. She ordered pie and a coffee. Ruby, the waitress, left with their orders.

Her mom didn't waste any time. "So…finally," she said. "Knox has finally seen you as a woman and you all finally did the deed. You've been waiting a long time for this."

That wasn't exactly what Trudie had expected.

"Mom!"

"Trudie." Harriet Brown laughed at her flummoxed daughter.

She'd had no idea her mom knew how she felt about Knox. "How'd you know?"

"Well, you're glowing and I've been your mother through all your relationships and you've never glowed before. I've known for a long time that Knox was the one who'd make it happen."

"But you never said anything."

"Neither did you, honey. But I knew he broke your heart after Mormor died and he turned to Elsa."

Ruby arrived with their drinks and Trudie's slice of lemon-meringue. "It was terrible, Mom."

She took a bite of the pie. Delicious. Lemony and tart, not too sweet.

Her mother echoed the phrase Trudie had used earlier. "But you never said anything."

"I didn't want you to worry about me. I knew you were already concerned about Knox and I didn't want to add to that. I had no idea you knew how I felt."

"You're my kid. I watched you and Knox grow up together and fall in love and neither one of you knew it. And I'm a woman. I just knew. So when did this... How did things change?"

Ruby showed up again—this time with Harriet's sandwich and chips. Trudie brought her mom up to speed while they ate.

Harriet pushed the last bite to one side on her plate. It didn't matter how hungry she was or how good the food was, Harriet Brown always left a bite. It was one of those quirks that used to drive Trudie crazy. Now she simply embraced it as her mom being herself.

"So, I guess we've got a wedding to start thinking about."

The idea both thrilled and terrified Trudie. Mostly terrified. "Uh, no. He hasn't asked."

"He will."

"I can't marry him, Mom."

"You're my child and I love you, but sometimes, Gertrude Ashland Brown, you confound me. Why in the world not?"

For the same reason she couldn't tell him she loved him last night. She simply couldn't bring herself to trust his feelings for her. "Mom, think about it. He was with Elsa for almost two years. He broke up with her maybe two weeks ago. I'm a rebound and you know you can't trust a rebound."

So, it was wonderful to be friends again, for the rest of the holiday, and being lovers had been fantastic last night and they'd have their romance, but Trudie had to think of it as a temporary thing, she had to hold back a part of herself. She couldn't...wouldn't tell him she loved him. She could go with what they had now, and when it ended it would hurt but it wouldn't devastate her. But if she really handed him her heart without reservation and he checked out on her again... she wasn't sure she'd ever recover.

"I agree...ninety-nine-point-nine percent of the time. You and Knox are that zero-point-one percent. You aren't a rebound for him. I think you both had to go your separate ways and lose what you just had to know what you had." Her mom paused a beat. "By the way...how was it?"

Hadn't her mom already told her she was glowing? "Wonderful." She wasn't about to go into any more detail than that, but she was definitely walking around with some great sexual buzz going on. And definitely looking forward to seeing Knox again this evening.

"Oh, good. I think I'll have a piece, too."

What...?

Her mother chortled. "Honey, you've definitely got a one-track mind today. The pie...I'm going to have a piece of pie."

Right. She was still looking forward to getting naked with him again tonight. And despite her mother's words, Trudie would keep her heart to herself.

9

KNOX WOKE UP the morning after the Chrismoose finale. Christmas Eve. Today they'd head back to Anchorage. Trudie was still snoozing. Even though she'd turned down his official offer to spend the week with him, she'd wound up spending her nights with him. He grinned. He couldn't think when he'd ever been happier…even without Mormor here. Neither had made any grand pronouncements, but he and Trudie had quietly gone to a couple of the events together. He'd had dinner with her folks a couple of nights. He hadn't been totally sure how Eldon and Harriet would take Knox and Trudie being lovers, but everything had been good. They welcomed him back into their family as if he'd never strayed—with open arms and warmth—much like a prodigal son.

Before they'd headed back late yesterday, Trudie's parents had invited him to join the family for Christmas dinner tomorrow. Knox had readily accepted. He did notice that Trudie remained quiet. She had, however, been a tigress in bed last night. They'd had very little sleep.

She blinked her eyes open.

"Morning."

"Morning." She sniffed delicately at the air. "I don't smell any coffee."

"You're spoiled."

"You created the monster, so it's your obligation to feed it. Coffee, please."

Laughing, he swung out of bed and padded naked into the kitchen. Jessup ran outside while he made the coffee. Their mornings had taken on a nice rhythm. He didn't want to give that up. He didn't want to give her up. Things were so good with them...surely she knew it, too. They were good together. He sensed—make that definitely felt—a reserve with Trudie that hadn't been there before, but then again they hadn't been lovers before.

Jessup whined at the door and he let the dog back in. Trudie climbed down the loft ladder, finally lured out of bed by the aroma of her morning brew.

"Thanks, Knox."

"Monster." He made a split decision, going with his gut. He reached under the tree and switched tags. He'd give her the earrings tomorrow.

He straightened, the small box in hand. "Today, I get mine first. Come on, hand it over."

She laughed but handed him his eleventh-day gift then sat on the couch. "See," he said, "I've obviously hung around you too much and your avarice for presents has rubbed off. You've created a monster as well."

"Apparently."

Knox opened the box. A miniature carving of a dog lay nestled in tissue. It easily fit in the palm of his hand and bore an incredible likeness to his pooch. "It's beautiful, Trudie."

"Well, now, even when you can't take Jessup with you, you can take his mini-me with you."

"Thanks, honey," he said, sitting next to her and hugging her.

"I'm so glad you like it. You're welcome." She held out her hand. "So..."

"Grubber."

"Am I a monster or a grubber? Make up your mind."

"How about a grubbing monster? And I'd like to make you mine."

A hint of wariness shadowed her eyes. "Mind."

He took the coffee cup out of her hand and placed it on the end table. "No, mine." He handed her the box but she simply sat and looked at it. "Open it."

"Okay." Her smile seemed strained. Instead of ripping off the bow and paper, this time she carefully dissected the wrapping job. He wasn't sure if she was stalling or she sensed that this gift wasn't like the others. Either way it didn't matter. He was still going to do what he was going to do.

She lifted the box lid and gasped. "Oh, Knox, it's absolutely exquisite."

"It reminded me of you the moment I saw it." She threw her arms around his neck and hugged him, pressing a kiss to his lips, but it was a chaste kiss.

"Let's see how it looks on," he said. He plucked the ring from the box and she handed him her right hand. Instead he took her left hand and slipped it onto her ring finger. "Perfect fit. And it looks great on you, too."

She was totally flustered. "It's very nice."

He could feel her retreating even though she hadn't moved but he was determined to stay his course. He'd lost his way once before and nearly lost her forever. He'd be damned if he'd risk that again.

He smoothed her hair back from her face and then cupped her cheek in his palm. "Marry me, Trudie. I love you. Jessup loves you. I've missed you. I don't want to miss you again. I want to wake up to your crazy hair and make you coffee every morning. I want us to have a couple of kids together and grow old together, still fishing and camping and doing what we do. You're not just my best friend, you're the love of my life."

Jessup, in a moment of good timing that made up for his bad timing earlier in the week, came and rested his head on Trudie's knee and gazed up at her as if to add his plea as well.

Trudie looked away from both of them. "Knox...I... This is so hard.... I just can't."

"Make me understand why you can't."

She wrapped her arms around her knees and rested her chin on them. "I think I finally understand what happened when Mormor died. You just couldn't be with me. But what if something tragic happens after we're married five, ten or even twenty years and once again you just can't be with me? I can't go through that again. And you and Elsa have only been broken up a couple of weeks. What if we don't even get five or ten years under our belt? What if a couple of months from now you figure out I was a rebound? I just can't, Knox."

"I don't know what to say to convince you, Trudie. You are definitely not a rebound and I will never walk away from you again."

She put her hand over her heart and tears glimmered in her eyes. "There's this reserve in here. It's not that I necessarily want it to be a part of me...of us...but it is. I can't love you body and soul, Knox."

She deliberately moved his ring to her right hand.

He felt as if she'd just ripped out his soul. And he could argue with her all day, but he'd known Trudie a long time and she had a stubborn streak a mile wide. They were at an impasse and there wasn't a damn thing he could do about it.

"Then I will wait. I'll wait until your soul comes out of lockdown. Hopefully, that's not years and years because I'd like for us to talk about a couple of rugrats before I'm too old to teach them to fish and cross-country ski and all the things we like to do together."

She pushed her hand uncertainly through her hair. "Knox, don't do this to me."

"Honey, the only thing I'm doing is giving you time...and asking you not to burn it all up before we're too old. Now, for the second order of business, are you going to help me take down this tree or what?"

She latched on to the subject change like a drowning man to a life raft. "I'll help with the tree."

An hour later the tree had been packed away, the cabin tidied and their luggage was in their respective vehicles. He walked her to her car. "Drive safe. And hey, do you mind if I still show up for Christmas dinner tomorrow?"

She wrapped her arms around him and leaned her head against his shoulder for a moment. "Of course not."

"I love you, Trudie."

She hesitated and then with a nod got in her SUV and was gone.

TRUDIE WALKED the last part of the trail with hope swirling through her. Christmas Day. She'd texted Knox, asking him to meet her at the park. She hadn't planned to head over to her parents' place until early afternoon so here she was. Snow crunched in the distance and she looked up.

Jessup and Knox crested the horizon. Love the man, love his dog. And she did. Both of them.

Silently they walked toward one another until they met halfway.

"Merry Christmas," she said.

"Merry Christmas," Knox said.

She handed Jessup a dental chew, which he promptly took and curled up with. He hated the snow, but he loved the green bones. She figured she owed her favorite pooch that much for dragging him out in the cold.

"Suck-up."

She shrugged. "I figured I owed him...ya know...the snow." She put her gloved hands in her coat pockets. It was a darn cold Christmas Day but she'd needed privacy and a neutral place to say what needed to be said and she'd rather foolishly and romantically always considered this to be their place. She fisted her hands in her pockets, fingering the ring through her gloves.

"I…uh…did a lot of thinking on the way home…"

"For goodness sake, Trudie, it's freezing…well, it's even more freezing than it usually is and you always just spit things out so just spit it out."

"I changed my mind. Well, my mind was convinced. I changed my heart. Well, I guess my heart was—"

"Trudie," he interrupted her. "Are you saying you will marry me?"

"Yes. Exactly. It's just you were rushing me."

He swept her up and pressed a hard kiss of promise on her lips and then released her. "I am one happy man, but let's walk and talk at the same time and carry this to the truck."

Her teeth were beginning to chatter in her head. She'd just wanted, needed, to tell him on this spot and she kind of sort of had.

Hand in hand they jogged lightly down the path back to where he'd parked his truck next to her SUV. They climbed into his cab and he started the engine.

"Say it," he demanded.

She thought about teasing him by saying how cold it was out there, but hearts on the line weren't teasing matters. "I love you, Knox. I think I've always loved you. I'm sure I always will."

"Body and soul?"

"Body and soul."

The dog between them, they kissed until they kissed the cold right out of their lips.

Jessup bumped them apart.

"I'm going to have to work with that dog," Knox said with

a happy grin. "I'm not looking a gift horse in the mouth, but what happened on that drive home yesterday that brought you around to my way of thinking?"

"I was just outside of Anchorage when the car ahead of me skidded out of control and hit a telephone pole. Luckily they weren't going too fast, and no one was hurt, but I thought it could've been me. Then I thought about the way I get in the car and drive almost every day but the odds are that I'm not going to skid out of control. Then I thought what if that driver never drove again because he was afraid he might get in an accident because it did happen to him once. You know what I mean?"

"I think I do. I hurt you but it would be pretty dumb to miss out on something that was wonderful because you were worrying about something that might, but probably won't, happen in the future."

He knew her, understood her in a way she didn't think anyone else ever would.

"I love you so much, it frightens me, Knox."

"I know, Trudie. I feel the same way."

She sighed and leaned in for a kiss. "On the twelfth day of Christmas my true love gave to me..."

He cupped her face. "Everything that's mine to give. All of me."

Joy, peace and goodwill flowed through her. So did desire. "We've got a little bit of time before we have to head to my folks'. If I trade places with Jessup, we could fog up your windows."

* * * * *

COMING NEXT MONTH FROM
HARLEQUIN® BLAZE™

Available December 18, 2012

#729 THE RISK-TAKER • *Uniformly Hot!*
by Kira Sinclair

Returned POW Gage Harper is no hero. He blames himself for his team's capture in Afghanistan, and the last thing he wants is to relive his story. But journalist Hope Rawlings, the girl he could never have, is willing to do anything to get it. Gage just might be her ticket out of Sweetheart, South Carolina—and what a hot ticket he is!

#730 LYING IN BED • *The Wrong Bed*
by Jo Leigh

Right bed...wrong woman. When FBI agent Ryan Vail goes undercover at a ritzy resort to investigate a financial scam at an intimacy retreat for couples, he'll have to call on all his skills. Like pretending to be in love with his "wife," aka fellow agent Angie Wolf. Problem is he and sexy Angie had a near fling months ago, and now the heat is definitely on while they share a hotel room—and a bed. Can they get through all those grueling intimacy exercises, all that touching and caressing...without giving the game away?

#731 HIS KIND OF TROUBLE • *The Berringers*
by Samantha Hunter

Bodyguard Chance Berringer must tame the feisty celebrity chef Ana Perez to protect her, but the heat between them is unstoppable, and so may be the danger.... Ana dismisses the threats at every turn, but she can't dismiss Chance or their incredible sexual chemistry. Soon the boundary between personal and professional is so blurred that Chance must make the hardest decision of all....

#732 ONE MORE KISS
by Katherine Garbera
When a whirlwind Vegas courtship goes bust, Alysse Dresden realizes she has to pick up the pieces and move on. Now, years later, her ex insists he'll win her back! Though she's curious about what's changed his mind, Alysse is reluctant to give her heart another chance, not to mention Jay Cutler. Still, she can't deny he's the one man she's never forgotten.

#733 RELENTLESS SEDUCTION
by Jillian Burns
A girls' weekend in New Orleans sounds like the breakout event Claire Brooks has been waiting for. But when her friend goes missing, Claire, who's always been on the straight and narrow, admits she needs the help of local Rafe Moreau, a mysterious loner. Rafe's raw sensuality tempts Claire like no other...and she can't say no!

#734 THE WEDDING FLING
by Meg Maguire
Tabloid-shy actress Leigh Bailey has always avoided scandal. But she's bound to make the front page when she escapes on a tropical honeymoon getaway—without her groom! Lucky her hunky pilot Will Burgess is there to make sure she doesn't get too lonely....

HBCNM1212ENHREVI

REQUEST YOUR FREE BOOKS!
2 FREE NOVELS PLUS 2 FREE GIFTS!

Harlequin *Blaze*

red-hot reads!

Bestselling Blaze author Jo Leigh
delivers a sizzling *The Wrong Bed* story with

Lying in Bed

Ryan woke to the bed dipping. For a few seconds, his adrenaline spiked until he remembered where he was. He groaned at the bright red numbers on the clock. "One a.m.? What…?"

The rest of the question got lost in the dark, but it didn't matter, because Jeannie didn't answer. His fellow agent on this sting must be exhausted after arriving late. "You okay?"

She tugged sharply on the covers, pulling more of them to her side of the bed.

Ryan could just make out her head on the pillow, her back to him, hunched and tight. Must have gotten stuck at the airport….

He curled onto his side, hoping to find the dream she'd interrupted. It had been nice. Smelled nice. He sighed as he let himself slip deeper and deeper into sleep…. The scent came back, a little like the beach and jasmine, low-key and sexy—

His eyes flew open. His heart thudded as his pulse raced. No need to panic. That was Jeannie next to him. Who else would it be?

Undercover jitters. It happened. Not to him, but he'd heard tales. Moving slowly, Ryan twisted until he could see his bed partner.

He swallowed as his gaze went to the back of Jeannie's head. Was it the moonlight? Jeannie's blond hair looked darker. And longer. He moved closer, took a deep breath.

"What the—" Ryan sat up so fast the whole bed shook. His hand flailed in his search for the light switch.

It wasn't Jeannie next to him. Jeannie smelled like baby powder and bananas. The woman next to him smelled exactly like…

She groaned, and as she turned over, he whispered, "No, no, no, no."

Special Agent Angie Wolf glared back at him with red-rimmed eyes.

"Jeannie is being held over in court," she snapped. "I'd rather not be here, but we don't have much choice if we want to salvage the operation."

She punched the pillow, looked once more in his direction and said, "Oh, and if you wake me before eight, I'll kill you with my bare hands," then pulled the covers over her head.

No way could Ryan pretend to be married to Angie Wolf. This operation was possible because Jeannie and he were buddies. Hell, he was pals with her husband and played with her kids.

Angie Wolf was another story. She was hot, for one thing. Hot as in smokin' hot. Tall, curvy and those legs…

God, just a few hours ago, he'd been laughing about the Intimate at Last brochure. Body work. Couples massages. *Delightful homeplay assignments.* How was this supposed to work now?

Ryan stared into the darkness. Angie Wolf was going to be his wife. For a week. Holy hell.

Pick up LYING IN BED by Jo Leigh.
On sale December 18, 2012, from Harlequin Blaze.

It all starts with a kiss

THE ONE THAT GOT AWAY

KELLY HUNTER

Check out the brand-new series

HARLEQUIN® KISS™

Fun, flirty and sensual romances.
ON SALE JANUARY 22!